The Stockton Insane Asylum Murder

A Portia of the Pacific Historical Mystery

Volume 3

JAMES MUSGRAVE

ISBN: 978-1-943457-38-0

Published by EMRE Publishing Fiction
San Diego, CA

Kirkus Review: Musgrave (*The Spiritualist Murders*, 2018, etc.) has some potent ingredients in this fantastical stew, spiced with many real-life figures, like Foltz, Toy, Galton, Kraepelin, and Elizabeth Packard, who helped reform commitment laws in the 1860s after being confined to an asylum when she questioned her husband's opinions. The setting is atmospheric and the subject, captivating.

The Stockton Insane Asylum Murder

By

James Musgrave

© 2019 by James Musgrave

Published by English Majors, Reviewers and Editors, LLC

An English Majors, Reviewers and Editors Book Copyright 2019

This novel is a work of fiction. Names, characters, places and incidents are the product of the author's imagination or are used fictitiously, and any resemblance to actual persons, living or dead, events, or locales is entirely coincidental.

English Majors, Reviewers and Editors Publishers is a publishing house based in San Diego, California.

Website: emrepublishing.com

For more information, please contact:

English Majors, Reviewers and Editors, LLC

JAMES MUSGRAVE

DEDICATION

We have come full circle. In the Nineteenth Century, insane asylums, for the most part, were prisons. Today, prisons, for the most part, are insane asylums. This book is for all those who have become victims of the continuing business of mental illness.

Acknowledgments

The women pictured, from left to right, Melissa Wilkinson, Jessica Adkins (at age 15), Sidney Reyes, Katherine Yantis, and Angela Thoma, won a raffle I held to feature them as characters and patients inside the Stockton State Insane Asylum in 1887. After they gave me personal information about their "crazy" idiosyncrasies, I crafted character outlines and then devised creative ways to include these new five characters in my mystery. This was quite a challenge to my imagination. I knew I not only had to create interesting and creative characters, but I also had to weave them into the plot of a mystery. However, after establishing a private group on Facebook, we were able to work together to compose and transform these fine ladies into Nineteenth Century insane asylum "lunatics." I have complete and signed permission from each woman to use their personal names and identities, although my fictional portrayals are a rather bombastic interpretation of their actual personalities. In fact, as I got to know them better on our book's social web page, I understood how much more interesting and beautifully diverse they were in "real life." Some are professionals working in challenging and rewarding occupations. Others have real experiences, including testifying at a murder trial, communicating with spirits inside haunted locations, and working hard at academic studies in college.

In fact, I truly believe the future of writing novels, especially historical novels, will contain the inclusion of readers in many ways, (see the recent "Bandersnatch" episode of the innovative Black Mirror series). The social media aspect of writing has progressed at full-throttle, and authors must find new ways of attracting their readers that allows them to participate uniquely in the entire writing process. Gone are the days of the lonely author, researching and pounding out his tome in utter solitude. Instead, today's savvy readers want more. They want to become involved right away. They even enjoy being participants in the author's creative process. Finally, they want to be able to act-out as characters inside an interesting mystery, and field questions from a waiting and eager public.

This is exactly what we'll be doing during our book launch, and continuing into the next book in my series, *The Angel's Trumpet*, in which a recent nominee to the 1887 United States Supreme Court is assassinated by a female and fanatical suffragette. This fictional nominee, Judge Marshal Owens, is a misogynist and womanizer, and Clara Foltz must defend his killer in a Washington D. C., much publicized trial.

Please join our social page to ask questions of these wonderful characters and the author.

Other Works by This Author

Interactive and Multimedia Enhanced eBooks

EMRE Publishing is now selling completely "enhanced" versions of its books through the unique Embellisher Multimedia Stream platform. Simply register inside the eReader to have access to the variety of titles. They contain relevant historical videos, music, interactive content, and a complete audiobook edition in many of the great titles.

Visit https://emrepublishing.com/new_embellisher-ereader/ to see what's available. Enter your email and a password to register and view. Buy your future digital copies of this Portia of the Pacific Historical Mystery series at reduced prices here: https://books.bookfunnel.com/portiaofpacific

"Madness can be seen as an intuitive probing into true reality."
--R. D. Laing

Table of Contents

Chapter 1: Undercover

The Women's Section, First Floor, Stockton State Insane Asylum, April 22, 1887.

There she was. Polly Bedford, age twelve, stooped-over in the shadows behind a row of bunk beds. Seated at a scarred wooden school desk, Polly was concentrating on her pencil drawing. She wore the patient's navy-blue frock pull-over with her initials "P.B." stitched on the left arm sleeve. Polly appeared to be drawing her residence inside the Women's Ward at the State Insane Asylum at Stockton. Her tongue tip was protruding from the corner of her mouth, and she kept pushing a strand of black hair back from her forehead, as she looked up from her tablet to view the interior of the ward.

As seventeen-year-old Bertha May Foltz walked up behind her, she could clearly see the bunk beds in the girl's drawing, the wash room, the dining room, and the windows, through which patients could observe their rural surroundings. Except, instead of creating people shapes--patients, doctors, nurses and visitors--Polly had colonised her mental ward with walking and talking medicine capsules. Each capsule, whether it was a patient or not, had stick arms and legs, and every face was drawn onto the top half of its pill torso.

Bertha, after reading the biography of Civil War Superintendent of Union Nurses, Dorothea Dix, became very interested in medicine. She would beg to go with her mother, Attorney and Detective Clara Foltz, every time one of her cases required that she visit the hospital or the coroner's office. When the homicide of ten-year-old Winnifred Cotton took place, just three doors down from where Bertha and her family lived in the mansion at One Nob Hill, Bertha decided she wanted to help her mother with the case. Not only was Polly Bedford a friend of Bertha's, she was also a member of the same choir that sang at Bertha's grandfather, Reverend Elias Shortridge's tent revivals at the sand lots on the Market Street side of San Francisco City Hall.

However, the secret reason Bertha wanted to help her mother was because her older sister, Trella Evelyn, and older brother, Samuel Cortland, had played important parts in the mystery the year before concerning the spiritualist murders. Bertha had watched them both as they pranced around the bedroom, claiming to have discovered this or that clue to contribute in the search for the killer. Samuel eventually broke the case wide open and was able to rescue their mother, Trella, and Samuel's future girlfriend, Adeline Quantrill, at the strange Sarah Winchester House in San Jose.

Bertha May realized that Polly Bedford's art was a probable reflection of the drugs she was being given to alleviate her high anxiety, such as potassium bromide, and to get her moving when she was in the valley of her melancholic despair, Strychnine. Of course, there was some wisdom in the girl's portrayal of drawn characters, as many of the staff could be seen, every night, slipping into the private suites on the top floor to sell cocaine, opioids, and even morphine to the wealthy female patients.

These rich patients never worked in the garden or on the farm. Instead, they stayed on the top floor, playing the piano, babbling incoherently about their paranoid suspicions, and grazing like lowing cattle at the ever-present collection of hors devours placed all around on tables inside their main dining room. They didn't have to sit at the main table downstairs with the poor patients.

In their drugged state, Bertha saw them to be the privileged insane, and every poor patient below, who was required to be shackled when not working outside, gave them envious looks when they spotted these women dancing, like ghosts, back and forth along the carpeted stairwells. They wore fashionable dresses with full bustles and ornate embroidery, and yet they acted like lunatics.

Bertha May was being supervised from San Francisco by her mother. Bertha was there to infiltrate the Stockton asylum, while pretending to be insane, with the sole purpose of questioning Miss Polly Bedford. Bertha was told by Clara that Miss Bedford had been committed by her parents because she had witnessed a murder which had taken place inside their residence, a stately mansion in the Nob Hill section of San Francisco. Clara also told Bertha that the Bedfords did not want Polly involved, and so they were willing to declare their daughter insane to keep her safe and legally out of the way. It was going to be Bertha's important job to discover who or what Polly saw on that night and to report back to Clara.

However, this case was much more complicated than the spiritualist murders. First of all, Bertha knew the murder witness, Polly Bedford. Bertha had played dolls and done homework with Polly, and Bertha had never found the younger girl to be belligerent or mentally strange. Therefore, Bertha was chosen by Clara to find out the identity of the person Miss Bedford allegedly saw commit this murder of Miss Winnifred Cotton, age ten, on January 3, 1887. If she discovered that Polly was not really insane, then she was going to explore how the institution was able to get so many people committed. However, Clara had explained to Bertha, at some length, she was not to steal or commit any crimes during her snooping adventure.

Bertha was going to see if she could determine what made this entire state asylum business run, and even though she knew her mother was looking out for her safety, Bertha was going to take all the risks she needed to accomplish her goal. If her brother, Samuel, could join the Tong Gang and spy on a spiritualist, then Bertha could be just as adventurous—perhaps even more so.

Her mother and the Cottons believed that mental illness was being sold as an easy way to get rid of troublesome wives and children and to secretly formulate a scheme whereby immigrants could be tricked out of their property and wealth by being committed. No money could come from the State of California to the State asylums at Stockton and Napa, unless the patients were ruled indigent.

Therefore, the same panel of doctors and state clerks was employed each year to do this nefarious business of separating the profitable wheat from the insane chaff, resulting in an incredible government statistic that said, "in 1886, alone, one out of every 435 Californians had been declared insane by the State." As this was an important women's and human rights issue, Clara and her team were motivated to uncover any illegal activities that might surface during their murder investigation. Bertha was overjoyed at being part of her mother's team at long last.

All Bertha knew before she was committed by her mother to the asylum was that Mr. Charles Cotton, President and Owner of the Cotton Gin Liquor Imports on Market Street, had deposited five hundred dollars into Bertha's personal bank account. Bertha was going to help her mother do what the City of San Francisco's Police Department was not permitted to do: find the killer of Charles Cotton's daughter.

"I have a new game we can play," Bertha spoke to Polly, sitting beside her chair, down on the lower bed of a nearby bunk ensemble.

Bertha watched the girl place her pencil down on the desk's top. She turned in her school chair and faced her older inquisitor. "Can we play Mental Metamorphosis again?"

It was as if an invisible force had sucked all the air out of the room. After the name of this game was released, the priority was now to breathe and to survive. Nothing else mattered. Bertha also understood what she must do. Using the girl's superior imagination and sensitivities to access her mind was a stroke of genius.

"Of course, we can," said Bertha, reaching out to capture the girl's hands in her own. "Instruction happens so much faster when the message can be implanted directly inside the brain. When you think, you are thinking for the collective good. Unless you control the actors, anything could happen, and that is the path toward chaos."

Polly moved out of her school chair and walked over to where Bertha was seated on the lower bed. Bertha knew this might be the only chance she got to obtain the information she needed. The staff was out supervising the farm and garden work of the others. Only kind old Mrs. Betterman, the baker, was left to mind the asylum, and she was almost deaf. Bertha set the stage immediately.

"What is the kernel of fear? We all have it, do we not?"

Polly stared straight ahead. "Not all. Some have no fear. They get trampled saving children and the elderly. Burnt to a cinder fighting Hell itself. Lost on the battlefields of the wars. I know one person who is the incarnation of Lucifer, the Fallen Star. I saw him murder an innocent. All the murderers are rejoicing. They at last have a hero on Earth to guide them."

Bertha spread out her dress with her palms, smoothing the material against her thin body. She was proud to be thin, and she thought her mother's weighty torso was unbecoming an active Suffragette for international women's rights. Back to her immediate concern, Bertha knew she needed more specific details about this Lucifer. "What did this demon look like? Certainly, he wasn't an apparition. You can't believe in ghosts."

A breathtakingly chilly vacuum devoured the space around them. Polly shivered, the first human reflex exhibited by her.

"You would pray there were ghosts, because no human could stop him. When he turned toward me, I saw his face was a continually changing compendium of different people's faces. I fantasized under stress about the possible reasons for this to occur. I may have eaten something horrid or poisonous. Or, supernaturally, I may have been put under a curse of some kind. Could I be an enemy of the government, who needed to be disposed of?" Polly's face became a bit animated, as she spoke, but her body remained rigid.

"What were you forced to do?" Bertha strained forward to take the girl's hands. "It's time to use your mental metamorphosis. If you become his mind, as he is in the act of killing a girl, tell me what you would be thinking and how you could change the reality of murder into something worthwhile and even redeeming."

The four times previously, when Bertha attempted to access Polly's mind, events kept occurring to interrupt the proceedings. Once it was an earthquake, once a fire alarm, and twice other patients had gone off the deep end and caused a ruckus. This was the moment Bertha had been long awaiting.

The eager smile on the girl's face demonstrated to Bertha that there were conflicting psychological forces at work. Polly, by all academic and social standards, was a genius child, a prodigy, but this turn of events had thrown the social welfare officials and newspaper journalists into an increasingly pessimistic state of conjecture. The idea that a girl's mind, especially a mind that came from such noble breeding, could be declared broken, was inconceivable.

Polly whispered, "I must stop the energy in this poor damsel. If she is allowed to grow older and breed, then the entire society is endangered. One small incision ..."

Bertha watched Polly's right hand. It was in the posture of holding a pen or perhaps a cutting utensil. She held it over something, her eyes focused upon the cutting motion being made by her empty but purposeful fingers.

"Polly, dearest. You may now metamorphose your brain and take control of his. What can you do to prevent this immoral act from occurring?"

As a result of public conjecture, Polly's existential reality was the daily emotional fodder for the masses. This or that doctor or nurse (whose efficacy was open to bidding) would secretly tell the press how the girl's parents were to blame and that no child can become insane without a direct influence from the parent figures. Other journalists would speculate that the government was behind a huge cover-up, and so many citizens were being adjudicated insane to keep them quiet. According to conspiracy fanatics, these inmates knew something, and they had to be kept silent.

Bertha could hear the commotion at the asylum's front entrance. The girls had returned from their labors in the garden and on the farm. She took hold of her chain and dragged the ten-pound steel cube across the room to her bunk. Bertha knew that the moment the workers came into the ward they, too, would have these shackles affixed to their legs.

One must always make it profitable for the state-run

institution, even if it means a little discomfort during enforcement. A recent statistical survey Bertha read had uncovered the fact that more patient accidents occurred because of there being no restraints, and the screaming dashes made by manic lunatics were not to be allowed. It was Bertha's goal, however, to lift the rock of outside speculation in order to explore the stark reality of the asylum's daily life, which was squirming from the mental disease called fear.

Chapter 2: The Home Fires

The Hopkins Mansion, One Nob Hill, San Francisco, April 23, 1887.

When the woman from the Stockton Insane Asylum came to the door, Samuel Cortland Foltz, nineteen, was playing cribbage with the butler, Hannigan. Samuel heard the voice of the woman, and he knew she was the attractive messenger paid for by his mother's suffragist friends. Samuel waved off the butler when he started to answer the door. The written epistle from his sister, Bertha May, would be handed to his mother, Clara Shortridge Foltz, Esq., and then the formal "Walk to the Library" would ensue. As Clara made her journey, inevitably, family members would begin to trail in after her until the chairs around the Library reference table were occupied, waiting for the grand reading by the attorney and leader of the investigative team.

Samuel was without his girlfriend, Adeline Quantrill. The eighteen-year-old psychic orphan, with whom he fell in love during the spiritualist murders case, was interviewing for a research post with Dr. Richard Lobe, the Ichthyologist, who worked directly for railroad millionaire, Leland Stanford. Samuel also knew Adeline was being used by his mother to investigate more closely into what their team was now referring to as the "Mad Money Exposé."

Five of the usual investigative members were there, and they were seated to Clara's right and left. On the right sat Clara's beaux, Captain of Detectives, Isaiah Lees, his usually serious demeanor being attacked by the jubilant woman next to him, Ah Toy, Clara's long-time friend and former Chinatown Madame. On Clara's left were her son, Samuel, her daughter, Trella Evelyn, and, down on the end, the owner and benefactress to them all, Mrs. Mary Hopkins, who seemed to be amusing herself by speaking for an improvised napkin puppet, which the old woman was bouncing against Trella's back. The young woman, used to the magical world of Mary's dementia, was not perturbed.

"Please, may we have some decorum? Or, I may be initiating immediate insanity hearings against Ah Toy and Trella Evelyn for having maniacal and fluctuating changes in their menstrual and uterine habits!"

All the women, except Mrs. Hopkins, began to guffaw loudly and strike the table with their fists or purses. Menstruation and uterine disease were listed reasons for women to be declared insane by California officials, as the group knew.

Clara pounded her fist louder. "Enough! I must now impart the reading." She turned to look down at Captain Lees. He was staring up at her like an Irish Setter at the feet of his mistress. "Go ahead. I know that pleading face. You have more information about our case from the city officials. We usually don't aspire to such lofty heights around here, but, go ahead, Isaiah. Tell us what you know."

Clara sat down and kept her eyes on Lees as he stood to address the gathering. He was wearing the outfit he wore on cases: a brown frock coat and vest with checkered pants and spit-shined Oxfords. Clara wished he paid as much attention to her as he did to his Oxfords, his guns, and the Bowie knife that he kept under his vest.

"Thank you, Madame Investigator. I am certain you are all familiar with our former mayor, and now California's governor, Mr. Washington Bartlett. In the first case Attorney Foltz took on, we had the mayor on our prime murder suspect list up until the last moment. He did, in fact, impede the investigation into the murders of eight women, for which he was never prosecuted." Lees nodded to Clara, who was waving at him.

"I want to get back to our present murder case. How is Governor Bartlett a factor?" Clara said.

Captain Lees was ready for that question. "I understand.

Governor Bartlett *is* connected to our present investigation. I just found out from his office, in fact, that the City of San Francisco will not be seeking any criminal grand jury indictment in the homicide of Winnifred Cotton, even though there is reason to believe the victim was pushed down the stairs and did not fall of her own accord."

"Winnie Cotton was a tomboy. She could out-wrestle and out-climb any boy her age. She would never trip." Trella Evelyn pointed out.

Lees continued, "It has also been resolved by the mayor's office that the commitment of Polly Bedford by her parents was legal and proper. Therefore, unless we can discover some evidence that gives us a witness at the scene of the girl's fall, or we get a sane confession from Miss Bedford as to this killer's identity, then Bertha May and Polly will have served their time in the asylum for nought."

Samuel decided to stand and deliver as well. "We began this inquiry when Polly's aunt, Mrs. Jeanne Forester, told mother that she overheard her sister, Louise, and her husband, Ronald Bedford, discussing the commitment of their daughter, Polly. The words Mrs. Forester heard were 'she can't be questioned by the police.' Now we have Bertha inside this asylum risking her life, and Adeline is away to infiltrate the halls of academe, while all we seem to be doing is laughing at suffragette humor."

Clara arose from her chair like an invigorated spirit of human rights. "Enough! We must focus on our present activities." She looked down at the report from her daughter at the Stockton hospital. It was the third such report since Clara had her strategically committed.

Samuel realized that his mother knew that her family and friends looked to her for guidance. They knew that Clara, along with fellow lawyer Laura de Force Gordon, had worked to get the law passed which accepted women into California law schools and gave women the right to enter any profession for which they were qualified. They also knew that Clara and her best friend, Ah Toy, were working to address the injustices of the intolerant culture that surrounded them. This case involved women and children being used as chattel in order to incarcerate them for free into mental asylums. These commitments were being done so the husbands or other relatives could profit, either directly or indirectly, from such confinement.

"Bertha May sends her love, and here is her report for this week. 'I was able to converse with Polly yesterday, but I believe the drugs they give her are dulling her senses and her intellect.' I shall now paraphrase." Clara looked up from the paper at her audience. "Polly describes the murderer of Winnie Cotton as being none other than Satan himself. No horns or other beastly persona for Miss Polly, however. Bertha says that, according to Polly, this devil murderer's face was a constantly moving display of different human faces. Polly also was certain this visitor was slicing into something just before the murder."

"The Great Liar lives amongst us!" Mrs. Hopkins shouted from the end of the table.

"From what my daughter says about the administration at Stockton, we can at least be assured of getting possible witnesses who will testify that they saw asylum staff selling narcotics to the wealthy female residents in the top floor suites." Clara, always looking for pathways of greed, had been taught well as to the motivation of corrupt persons, especially those who work for the government.

Both her father Elias Shortridge, and her lover, Captain Lees, had in the past been arrested for disobeying arbitrary laws meant to protect the corrupt overseers. And, as the Women's Suffrage Movement also knew, females were seen as the weaker sex for a reason. Without the ability to get out of the home in order to pursue her calling, a woman was also an institutionalized citizen, ripened for the plunder.

Ah Toy raised her hand, and Clara nodded at her. She seemed very poised in her red silk *cheongsam*. Her English was eloquent and well pronounced. "Back in China, the Manchu would have workers join committees that were supposed to root out favoritism and corruption, but the rulers used that information to arrest those who would blame others. In China, if you were

20

committed, it usually meant you would die. In this country, it seems, the institutionalization of humans can mean a profitable enterprise for those who can play the game well."

It was eldest daughter Trella Evelyn's turn to raise a hand. She was wearing the newest female liberation attire, a black gabardine suit, with a crimson tie hanging down belligerently between the breasts, and no preposterous bustle or python girdle to impede the free movement of a woman with a purpose. "I believe Ah Toy has a brilliant idea, even though she has not voiced it. Mother, you have always remarked that ideas are there for anybody to seize, but it is the enlightened person who steals these ideas and puts them into motion."

"Please, Trella dear. Get to the point," Clara said.

"We should form a citizens' committee to investigate the goings-on at Stockton," Trella said, rising slowly to her feet, as her voice gained volume and confidence. "Mrs. Hopkins and her friends certainly have the wealth and political influence to coordinate such a bi-partisan effort. We should keep it away from our suffrage connections, lest the men see through us to our ultimate goal."

Clara wanted to give her daughter a bit more rope so she could hang herself properly and lady-like. "And what, pray tell, is our ultimate goal?"

"Why, to arrest every member of that corrupt male system in California that makes us the laughingstock of the nation. More Californians are being committed to mental hospitals than in any other state of the union. People are committed for being drunk in public, having hysterical menstrual cramps, and being insane for not speaking English." Trella's neck was red with emotion.

Clara was waiting for her daughter's voice to register near the soprano pitch sung in a Wagnerian opera. There it was. "All right. That's enough! I appreciate your fervent devotion to justice, Trella, and the idea is good, but the elaboration is not. For us to initiate such a committee, we will need an extremely decorous and judicial approach. Uncontrolled emotions, as you should all be aware, are the Achille's heel of our movement. Many other women are against the female right to vote because women are important to

21

the home fires. Without a woman's intelligent touch, so goes the logic, a home can quickly degenerate into chaos and fear."

Samuel watched his mother gather steam. He had witnessed this often. The unfathomable power of eloquent argument.

"Don't look at me that way, Ah Toy. You know as well as I that without your sexual allure, you would have never made it out of Chinatown alive. Therefore, we shall form a very prudent, sober, and un-biased committee to investigate Stockton State Insane Asylum. We shall base our inquiry on very specific allegations, and our members will represent a cross-section of the community—both male and female—and our purpose will be to protect the best interests of all California taxpayers and citizens."

Captain Lees stood up. "You need a member of the legal establishment to sit on this committee. I know a retired judge who would agree to such an appointment."

Clara turned toward him. "Yes, and father can give us an esteemed reverend from the Christian community. Do we have anybody from academia and labor?"

"I have a professor at Berkeley who can serve. He teaches History and is well respected by his fellow researchers." Trella Evelyn was in college, and Samuel expected she would recommend that professor. She also thought he was dreamy and handsome.

Ah Toy raised her hand and waited until Clara nodded at her. "Chinatown is constantly working to gain advantage in our competitive economy. I believe it would be proper to include a labor official of Chinese descent on our committee. I know of one such respected official, and she is willing, I am certain."

"Thank you, Ah Toy. We now have a framework for our new investigative committee. Obviously, we will need to interview these new appointees, and each of you who spoke will coordinate together to schedule our interview. Be reminded. We are not out to save the world. As of this moment, our task is to prove a little girl has been murdered. Whatever crimes may branch outward from this central search are not of our immediate concern. With God's help, we have members in our international movement who will step in when needed to bridge the gaps."

Samuel knew they would end the meeting with applause. As he joined in, he thought about Adeline. Would she become more motivated by the pull of academic research so that she soon forgot about him? He really had no immediate plans. He still gambled in Chinatown, somewhat successfully. His mother's practice and "The Law" were on his distant horizon perhaps.

Samuel also thought about his sister, Bertha May. He knew that part of Bertha's motivation was to prove she was equal to he and Trella. He and Trella knew the real danger Bertha was in, and the excitement of her adventure exceeded the risk by microcosmic proportions.

He, along with their entire investigative team, knew they would now proceed carefully. The motivation to serve the common good was to always be at the forefront of any investigation they pursued. There was something about that last statement that always made Samuel's chest swell with pride.

***

The Cotton Mansion, Six Nob Hill, San Francisco, California, April 23, 1887.

Clara was in relatively good spirits when she walked through the garden leading up to the Cotton home, five doors down from Mary Hopkins' mansion. She had given direct instructions to her team about how they would collect information in the coming days. Of course, her daughter Bertha was in danger, but unless the murderer were inside the asylum, the risk could be kept to a minimum. Clara believed, of course, in the higher good. Humans needed something to look forward to as well as something to appreciate immediately. Without hope, humanity was doomed.

A tall butler took her shawl and parasol, and Clara adjusted her auburn hair and straightened her new teal hat. The silk teal dress and moderate bustle served as assisting decorations in this important tête-à-tête. The most important task to Clara was how to decorate the questions she was about to ask this special person. She knew just how important it was to have an audience with Mrs. Elizabeth

Packard, a woman who, in the 1860s, had been committed to an insane asylum for three years. Like Clara, she was a single mother with six children. Mrs. Packard won her case against the patriarchal authorities, and she turned to the law, in order to enact changes to reform state policies on housing and caring for its mentally ill population. Clara was meeting a woman who had established a national association of experts to address the changes needed at mental asylums in all the states.

As she followed the maid through the mansion, Clara noted how her senses were being distracted away from the usual garish antique furnishings, pungent exotic incense, and even the artwork collections. When one lived inside the beast of capitalism, the opulence quickly became commonplace, especially if one was engaged in legal conundrums that had to do with civil rights for women, the lesser races, foreign cultures, and other lower classes.

Winona Cotton was, of course, still wearing mourning black for her daughter, Winnifred, whose death was the proximate cause of this arranged meeting between Clara and Mrs. Packard. Her eyes were bright, and her hands were warm as she grasped Clara's. "Come. Let me introduce you to her right away. My friends and I, quite naturally, will be leaving the room the moment you give the word. I must tell you. She does have one affectation at age seventy-one. She won't use a hearing apparatus, so she will often not hear you well. You must speak louder than you would normally speak for her to hear you."

Clara nodded and followed her hostess into the study off to the side of the main dining room. Ever the good detective, Clara was making mental notes about the identities of the persons she knew who were inside that study. There was only one personage she did not recognize, a slender man with fashionable mutton-chop sideburns warming his cheeks and framing his blue-eyed gaze. The others were Charles Cotton, Winona's husband, and Clara's close attorney friend, Laura de Force Gordon. Clara assumed Laura was there representing the Cotton family, as she had also represented them during the formal inquest into the cause of Winnifred's death. Laura had been of great assistance in Clara's second case, last year, helping to capture the spiritualist who was responsible for women killing their husbands.

Then, there was the woman Clara really wanted to meet. Mrs. Elizabeth Ware Packard wore a plain, rural dress of dark blue with a white lace apron tied around her middle. The plaid shawl encircled her rather wide shoulders, and the cameo brooch under the white blouse at her neck complemented her calm and inquisitive gray eyes. Her wispy white hair was loose and about her shoulders, and there was something about the way Mrs. Packard leaned forward as Clara approached, and smiled beneath her white bonnet, which caused Clara to say the following to the older woman in a loud voice.

"I trust you are not wearing a corset, Mrs. Packard, lest your father and ex-husband commit you again for purposely cutting off the proper flow of blood to your weak, female brain." Clara took the woman's spotted hands into her own and peered deeply into her intelligent eyes. She at once saw the elder's eyes light up with good humor as she squinted, smiled, and nodded at Clara.

"Ah, Mrs. Foltz. At last, someone who understands the role that simply being of a different sex can mean to one's ability to work and to even breathe comfortably. I keep telling my so-called followers that they need only begin a revolt in the bedroom to get things changed the way they should be. That would most certainly include our women who do their wifely duties in the bordello. Certainly, you'll agree, Aristophanes was onto something when he wrote *Lysistrata*. Women of today simply do not have the gumption to follow the Greek women's plan through. If the corset were on the men's bodies, these gallivanting troubadours of ours would become celibate monks. Just to win a drunken wager at a tavern house, they thought they could escape this mighty garment-python's grip. It is we women who need to gird our loins and, if you'll pardon the expression, herd our collective and closed loins, to put a stop to intolerant male behaviors."

"Oh yes, Mrs. Packard . . ." Clara began, chuckling and sitting down next to her on the davenport. She motioned to her friend Laura to sit down at the end as well, and she did.

"Please, do call me Elizabeth, or even Liz, if you're of the modern set. You must be, as you're so young and flirtatiously attractive." Mrs. Packard adjusted a curl that was sticking down too far on Clara's wide forehead. At thirty-eight, with five children and a robust figure, Clara believed Liz may also need spectacles.

"I'm sorry to be in such a rush. I must be off to another round of questioning in this matter. May we begin? I understand attorney Gordon will be staying to represent the Cotton family's interest in these proceedings. That will be fine, but we need to clear the room of everyone else." Clara glanced around, first at Mr. and Mrs. Cotton and then at the strange gentleman. She made a mental note to later ask Laura who he was. After she watched them exit the study and close the double-doors behind them, Clara turned once again to yell at Mrs. Packard.

"Let me attempt to summarize my predicament at this juncture, Liz," she said, deciding on incorporating the familiar name for this great woman, as it would assuage Clara's own fears of sitting right next to this noble champion of human rights.

"By all means, Attorney Foltz. And, welcome, Mrs. Gordon. I am aware of your courtroom battles to defend the rights of women, some of whom, I might add, were railroaded into mental institutions for the profit of their husbands or other family members." Mrs. Packard folded her hands into her lap. "Certainly, in my own case, back in the 1860s, there were no means of protection to stop the abuses, but now we at least have some protection and even overseers, although law and enforcement are two very different realities, as I'm certain you're both aware."

Clara noted that Laura again wore her plain, dark blue work attire, which reflected her affinity for the masses. No bustle, no frills, and certainly no feminine allure. Whereas Clara used her own grace and feminine stylishness to catch the male opposition off-guard, it had been Laura's strategy all along to come at her opponents with rhetorical guns blasting away, with no regard for a fashionably attractive personal appearance.

Laura Gordon was an efficient and practical San Francisco lawyer, whereas Clara had always tried to look at the big picture, even at a state and federal level, and to plan accordingly. All three of them, Clara knew, had one thing in common. They had all been jilted by husbands who believed women were there to serve them and not there to rebel against their ironclad power.

"Liz, we don't have the membership or far reach that you and your fine organization have. This does not mean our present case warrants your attention out of hand. It does not. Instead, I propose an affiliation based on the understanding that we wish to change the entire mental health care system and not the patients or the people working within. The system must always accommodate the best interests of the individual, whenever possible, with the understanding that organizations must have discipline and order in order to function."

Mrs. Packard was mumbling some words to herself and nodding.

Clara gasped. "Liz?" she said, at a greater volume, remembering about the elder's hearing impairment. "Did you hear anything I just said?"

"I'm sorry, my dear. No, I really did not hear one word. I am fortunate to have you here today. I must remember to tell friends to speak louder when in my company. This is what they called in the asylum a breakthrough, Mrs. Foltz." Mrs. Packard leaned back and sighed. "Sadly, our society often supports isolation and eccentricity, when it comes to research and intelligent scientific and even religious speculation. However, you must always do this under society's auspices, because we all know there is supposedly no such thing as an isolated genius. Without the kiss of approval from society, a genius may as well be a mad person raving, within an asylum, squatting in the corner, excrement in his hands, nude, and with no hope or belief in God or for the future."

"We need your understanding of how things actually function inside these asylums," Clara was almost shouting, and she noticed that Laura was wincing from the sound. In their courtroom debates, Laura was always the loud one, who could make a jury sit up and listen. Clara, on the other hand, would always come near. Nearer to the judge, to the jury, to the witness. Her speaking method was to fabricate intimate secrets, whereas Laura's technique was to compete directly with the men.

"You have achieved a life about which most women merely dream, Mrs. Foltz. Other women do not realize, of course, that the reality of being given some access to the patriarchal authorities is no guarantee that they will listen. That is when we females use our hidden talents of the supernatural variety, is it not?"

Clara nodded and smiled. She was thinking about the young psychic, Adeline Quantrill, whom she employed to ferret out the identity of a murderer, and who was now being courted by Samuel, Clara's son. The girl was presently applying to assist one of the most prominent and influential families in America, the Stanfords. This bastion of academic exclusivity would be quite surprised to discover that Clara and her investigative team had planted Adeline there to spy on them.

"Some might call madness the isolated genius of a Jesus, a Mohammed, or a Buddha," Mrs. Packard continued. "Or, others might call it the madness of a mind gone off its trolley. I thought I would use that metaphor, as those monstrosities you have going up these Sisyphus hills may as well be circumnavigating between heaven and hell, or mania and melancholy."

"What is your biggest fear about what can happen when society allows the subjugation of human beings for the purposes of isolation away from more respectable members of the community?" Clara hoped her open-ended question would allow Mrs. Packard the freedom to explore her innermost beliefs based on her horrendous personal experience and battle to survive.

"Make no mistake. There are those mental patients who are quite a danger to themselves and to others. They should be the focus of attention at these facilities. Why? They need proper care aimed at preventing physical harm. Whereas, much of the political shenanigans we face have to do with the manipulation of innocent minds for profit, I am quite pleased to be part of your investigation, Mrs. Foltz. My organization and I often become too distracted from the daily realities of our entire society. We become so riveted upon the noble quest to release innocent minds from captivity that we ignore the one true way we can actually cause change. We cannot uncover conspiracies within the organization which point to an evil trend in the very process of caring for the mentally ill. I am proud to serve you in this regard because this is what you will be doing."

A young red-haired woman wearing a nurse's dress rushed into the room, and Clara was at first angry at the interruption, as she had just begun to appreciate Mrs. Packard's acceptance and what it meant to her plans. Luckily, the visiting nurse was talking to Laura Gordon, as she was seated as the closest of the trio to the entrance. After a few moments of intense whispering, back and forth, Laura got up and walked over to Clara.

"She's the messenger from Stockton. She says Polly was confined to isolation. It seems when a fellow patient shared in open discussion about how she knew Miss Bedford to be a secret spy for the government, Polly rushed at the woman and attempted to gouge her eyes from their sockets, or so the written report reads."

Clara felt her heart clutch in her breast. Could someone in that state-employed community have discovered that Polly was connected to Bertha May? And, upon further inside investigation, perhaps they found out that Clara and her group were behind Bertha being committed. It was one of Clara's worst nightmares as a sleuth. That moment when you have discovered that your adversary was one step ahead of you, as you were about to pull the magician's screen back to reveal the real culprits behind the sorcery.

"I have worked to pass thirty-four state bills which directly address these problems. Most often, the guilty party has been discovered by using common sense and an application of human and Christian values. However, in some circumstances, there was a malfeasance committed against a patient that demonstrated evil and even murderous intent. At those moments, I am very happy to turn the authority to investigate over to an honest and caring legal professional, such as yourself." Mrs. Packard nodded at Clara.

Clara smiled over at Laura, who nodded back at her. "We completely agree with you, Mrs. Packard. Even though my own daughter could be in jeopardy, I will not jump to any conclusions before we can hear all of the witnesses to this event. Are you at liberty to travel with us to the Stockton asylum? On the way, I can tell you about the citizens' committee we are in the process of forming in order to thoroughly investigate the entire administration and its staff. We believe this will lead directly to discovering the person or persons responsible for the death of Miss Winnifred Cotton."

"Even during my darkest times inside the Illinois asylum, I was never treated as badly as when I was placed under the roof of my own husband. He locked me up and would not allow me to socialize with anyone. This is what drives one authentically insane. The reality that you are not allowed the privilege of being with fellow humans."

Laura added to the conversation. "Indeed. Isolation recently killed one of my clients. She could not stand her seclusion and committed suicide with purchased drugs she procured on the prison's black market."

Mrs. Packard continued with her memoir, and Clara noted that her complexion became flushed as she spoke more vehemently than before.

"When I was in the asylum, at least I could talk to other women, and we understood how we were being treated, because our every waking moment was monitored by our caretakers. This was not a democracy, but my asylum treatment did not come close to the way the government had bequeathed my husband with the power to imprison me. According to my Christian religion, my Calvinist caretaker should have obeyed the obligation to protect his wife and not to imprison her. We must get that Bedford girl out of isolation!" Mrs. Packard concluded, and she stood up.

Chapter 3: The Intent of the Insane

Central Pacific Train to Stockton, April 23, 1887.

Clara wanted to use this inquiry into Polly Bedford's alleged assault upon another resident as a way to insinuate their investigation into the life blood of the state asylum's daily activities. Mrs. Packard had already wired the superintendent at the Stockton asylum with instructions to take Polly out of isolation until they arrived.

It was as if this change in circumstance had opened up a new method to eavesdrop, with careful planning, into the heart of murderous intent itself. As an attorney-at-law, Clara understood that most crimes of passion, of which murder was the most heinous, had to be proved in front of a jury, beyond any reasonable doubt, that the Defendant's action was intentional and deliberated upon before he or she made a move.

Along the Central Pacific route toward Stockton, inside their cabin, Clara was able to discuss, albeit at an increased volume, with Elizabeth Packard and Laura Gordon, about why their investigation centered around the murder of Winnifred Cotton. Also, how they needed to prove an intent that went far beyond that of a single murderer's state of mind. Clara was relaxed as she spoke, and she would often turn in her private first-class seat, to gaze out at the passing farm land as they journeyed, the coach swaying, the rails click-clacking like the castanets of a Spanish dancer.

"You see, that's why I wanted my daughter, Bertha May, committed to the asylum. She believes her friend, Polly Bedford, is not insane at all. It's her idea that the administration has been instructed, by whom we know not, to give Polly drugs to keep her in a confused state of mind. I propose we inquire into that area. When an actor is under duress or has been drugged, either voluntarily or involuntarily, his or her actions are not to be considered intentional." When she saw Laura's eyebrow raise, Clara nodded for her to speak.

"Yes, and intent works both ways, my dear. If you believe there is some nefarious conspiracy of a group, then you have the burden of proving intent on their part, as well as showing that each member of that conspiracy took an advanced step toward completing the illegal action, even a murder." Laura shook her dark-brown hair, and Clara remembered that same glint of satisfaction in Laura's eyes that she saw so often during their trials opposing each other in a court of criminal law.

Clara smiled, choosing to circumvent her friend's challenge for the moment. "Naturally, under the present legal circumstances, Miss Bedford has been ruled insane. Thus, her civil rights are completely obliterated. If she is insane, then her intent is nullified, but the same goes for her actions if she were not insane. Why? Because if she is not insane, then the drugs being administered to her for her diagnosed insanity are not warranted. Therefore, the intent of her actions while under the influence of illegally prescribed drugs, is also negated, because she was not lucid."

It was Mrs. Packard's turn to smile, and Clara was so expectant that she reached out and took the older woman's hand.

"What you say is clear," Mrs. Packard said. "It also suggests that you need another expert to add. You need a physician who works daily with committed patients and who can speak with the utmost authority about how drugs affect a patient's mind and body. Most importantly, he must know if their dosage can mitigate intent in the human mind."

"Thank you, Liz. Do you really have a doctor in mind who would do this?" Clara asked.

"I certainly do. He played an important role in my own investigations, when we were attempting to impose pharmaceutical regulations upon several state mental asylums across the country.

He traveled with me to seventeen hearings in eight different states. His name is Dr. Andrew McFarland, and he was the superintendent in charge of the Illinois State Asylum for the Insane, in Jacksonville, where I was when I challenged the authorities about my own illegal internment by my husband." Mrs. Packard straightened her collar.

"Is he sympathetic to your cause?" Laura shouted.

"Sympathetic? Well, he quit his employment as the superintendent, due to what we proved was going on under his nose, and he established a private hospital, Oak Lawn Retreat, where he now works as the Superintendent and Assistant Physician. However, I must point out, he will not come to us without the accompaniment of his constant companion, and apple of his eye, his granddaughter, Anne."

"Still another member to join the fray?" Clara raised her eyebrows but smiled. "I suppose having an extra woman will also help us."

"Indeed, it will. I don't know how many times Andrew has informed me he plans to base his entire mental health program for women around his mentally and physically fit granddaughter, as he believes she will make a superb doctor. She will be entering medical school beginning in the new term."

"She is getting quite a special education with her grandfather serving as mentor," Laura shouted.

"Indeed. Anne becomes quite vehement when we discuss the current practice of blaming female mania and nervousness on the patient's menstrual and gynecological disorders. She will instruct you, in the minutest details, about how this policy was instituted in order to reap thousands of dollars from the coffers of every pharmaceutical, gadget, and uterine gimmickry manufacturer known to Man." Mrs. Packard took a deep, resigned breath.

"I can't speak for my entire team, but I believe these two experts will be excellent additions. I want to thank you, Liz, for your assistance. When can they be in California to help us?" Clara's voice was still loud, and she squinted as she spoke.

"Good. Then I shall wire them through Western Union when we arrive in Stockton. They should make it out here in three days, if all goes well. We certainly won't be able to secure a date for our first committee investigation for at least three days, don't you think? That's been my experience in other states. This is the first time I've taken on the system in California. Do you believe it will be difficult?" Mrs. Packard's eyes were glowing with enthusiasm.

Both Clara and Laura were smiling roguishly at that question. Clara spoke first. "California began Stockton's existence in controversy. The first superintendent, a Dr. Reid, was accused in court of using patients as slave labor to add furnishings and a new garden to his personal home. He was also accused of underreporting deaths and using single graves for multiple burials. His trial, begun by the governor, ended in Reid being discharged."

Laura shouted, with her hands circled around her mouth. "Yes, and two doctors—one sympathetic to Reid and the other to the governor—fought a duel over the testimony given against Reid by another doctor who later, coincidentally, became the new superintendent. Luckily, the wounded man, Dr. Langdon, received only a fractured leg when the bullet struck him. As you can see, Mrs. Packard, stories in the penny press about our life in the Wild West are not always exaggerated."

"And, since you speak of aboriginal thinking, what is the overall philosophy at this asylum? Does it accede to the current trend in blaming the body for the condition of the mind? Misogyny, as I have discovered, time and again, often lies at the heart of the way the women are treated inside these state facilities." Mrs. Packard struck her breast with her fist.

"From what we've studied, California mental health authorities subscribe to the theory that social stressors cause mental illness. Allegedly, our Gold Rush and our increasingly complicated industrial society affect our population—many of them from foreign lands—in very negative ways." Clara held her arms out wide. "The cure, so to speak, is for the asylum to be a grand place where the patient can relax, in rural splendor, in order to be treated for mental problems caused mostly by social stress and physical ailments. Thus, we have the water method of keeping a patient's body invigorated by warmth and liquid, thus clearing the mind for more logical thinking."

"Go ahead, Clara, I know you're going to say it," Laura remarked, frowning.

Clara nodded at her friend and smiled. "Yes, and I was especially enthused when you mentioned Miss Anne, the granddaughter of Dr. Andrew McFarland. We have reason to believe these conspirators—perhaps even the murderer him or her self—are profiting from misogynistic practices as well as from the old-fashioned crimes of embezzlement of government funds and outright torture."

Laura snapped back, "The State of California does, in fact, have a very mixed population, and as we know, it is also a very difficult society in which to succeed. Our citizens are under constant threats from labor unrest, we treat our immigrants with disdain, and we move the mentally ill away from these stressors so they can be cured of the mostly attitudinal problems they develop. Attorney Foltz here seems to forget that many upstanding citizens, such as my clients, the Bedfords, need a safe place to commit their obviously insane children. And, the drugs and daily physical regimen are here to assist in medical treatment and not here to aggravate the problem of the patient."

"Oh, it can get quite aggravated when profit becomes a cure, and drugs become the snake oil for the State's coffers," Clara said, and her eyes became livid. She met her fellow attorney's stare with equal resistance.

"As we always say, Counselor, that will be determined in court." Laura adjusted the black comb in her hair. Because Clara was a personal friend, Laura was obviously holding back on her usually antagonistic rhetoric. If they were inside a courtroom, Clara knew, Laura's talons would be showing.

***

This was the third visit for Clara to the Stockton State Insane Asylum. But it was the first involving her daughter, Bertha May, and her companion, Polly Bedford. As they rode out to the institution by rented horse and buggy, Clara reflected upon how different she and Laura Gordon were in one key area of the law. The insanity defense. Clara believed not being able to determine right from wrong was solid proof that the perpetrator did not have the requisite intent. Laura, in opposition, believed only the perpetrator could know about state of mind at the time of the act, so because there was no objective viewpoint from which to judge, there could be no mitigating circumstance of insanity. Judges could not be mind readers and neither could alienists.

Clara enjoyed the sensory panorama riding on the train. The rivers of the California Delta swirled around them. Waves of different odors wafted into the coach: onion, fertilizer, flowers, fruits and many more indescribable and pungent smells. As both Mrs. Packard and Laura were eating fresh peaches, sold from a cart during their trip, Clara reached over and grabbed one from the bag between them.

As she smelled the unique odor of the peach, Clara realized how nonsensical it was to determine the guilt or innocence of a human being upon subjective and often intolerant human reason. According to the patriarchal authorities, one cannot be conscious of one's actions unless one can reason. The animals, even the primates, do not write down their histories and memories. These creatures do not explore the universe nor do they understand the laws of a society created for their own interests.

Ironically, the so-called "insane" person could reason. True, their reasoned world was usually an inner society based completely upon personal and not societal tastes, and on subjective, idiosyncratic status symbols rather than on social whims. Who could truthfully say which reason was superior? If the insane person were kept in the attic, inside an elite mansion, sleeping in satin, prattling to servants, getting featured at Christmas like the other poor oddities in life, then the intent and actions of the insane person were producing a positive result. The insane person's inner society was not part of the outside, and yet it still existed. It was only the social communications network that was missing in this equation.

If the insane person were protected by outside society, then could he or she live another day, without harm, and with a possible hope for the future? For example, in the case of Mrs. Mark Hopkins, Mary, Clara's wealthy benefactress, the old woman's dementia was being protected by Clara's legal knowledge and by Ah Toy's administrative abilities. Without their protection, the old woman could easily be committed to an asylum by unscrupulous types, who had no other concern other than reaping profits from the railroad heiress's formidable estate.

Clara knew that each day was perhaps her last chance to find the connections between that inner, sometimes insane world, and that outer, perhaps eternally insane world. In those moments of breakthrough, when the sick, insane mind sees it is being heard and is being accepted as a legitimate reality, will insanity become open to criticism and possible cure?

Clara also knew this honorable treatment of humans, such as what Mrs. Packard advocated, was at the heart of her own goals as an attorney. Many societal labels were meant to categorize and isolate you from the elite, mostly prosperous, citizens. Status and biased labels, in contrast, were created for both the elite rulers and the poor workers. However, the elite controlled the message propaganda and the enforcement of the rules. The "rub," as Shakespeare would call it, was that the ruling class in 1887 saw most of existence as an extension of themselves: a business.

The name of the gentleman with the lamb-chop side-whiskers, present at the Cotton Mansion inquiry, was Dr. Alfred Rooney, the present Superintendent of the Stockton Insane Asylum. Laura passed that information on, when Clara asked her in the middle of a discussion of the men Laura was seeing romantically. It was a tactic that Clara often used whenever she wanted information from her friend. Laura's mind became so fixated upon making whatever she was explaining correct that she would often answer almost any inquiry with complete honesty.

"My clients want him to be present whenever there is any questioning by any authorities. The Bedfords are on the California State Board of Advisors to the Health and Education Committee. Obviously, they cannot risk any misinterpretation of facts when it concerns the policies at Stockton asylum." Laura's brown eyes were hooded by what Clara called her "focus frown."

"My, that is quite resourceful of you, Mrs. Gordon," Clara said. She knew her good friend did not enjoy being called by her married title. Clara used her own marriage title to protect her and her five children and their social reputations. Clara told society she was a widow when, in fact, she was divorced because of her husband's desertion.

Laura, on the other hand, never had children, and her previous husband was a philanderer. Even though they were both deserted by their husbands, as was Mrs. Packard, it was Laura who came out of the experience angrier. In Clara's opinion, Laura now used men as a soothing balm for her Free Love tendencies, whereas Clara had chosen to remain monogamous and single with the Captain of Detectives, Isaiah Lees, as her lover.

As they neared the steps leading up through the archway into the main admittance room, Clara looked up. The sun was now descending behind the top steeple, shining its weakened rays through the bell tower. Hundreds of fluttering bats were streaming out, like a burst of dark thoughts, and Clara shivered, reaching up to hold onto her hat in the breeze.

There was an ominous foreboding all around her, and even the cooking odors of potatoes and lamb could not assuage the fear the attorney felt deep inside. It was as if a curse had already been placed on this residence, and what they were actually doing was going through a strange ritual meant for all of those who would dare question the human motives behind this portentous cathedral of darkness.

As they walked up to the entrance, on the shadowy grounds of the women's side of the rather eerie Gothic structure, Clara decided to probe a bit more deeply into Laura's legal preparations. Perhaps she knew how the politicians on this advisory board addressed official explorations into conduct that may have led to an assault by one of its residents. Upstairs, a woman screamed, just as Clara and her group entered.

***

The Women's Section, First Floor, Stockton State Insane Asylum,
April 23, 1887.

"Thank you, Superintendent," Clara said, sitting directly across from Dr. Rooney inside the asylum's staff conference room. They were adjacent to his personal office on the ground floor's admission area. Alfred Rooney was alone, as his staff was stretched thin, caring for the over five-hundred female residents. "I have with me Mrs. Elizabeth Ware Packard. I would expect you are aware of her special expertise. She has agreed to assist me in this committee investigation of the event concerning Polly Bedford."

The young superintendent shuffled some papers in front of him, cleared his throat, and stared directly at Mrs. Packard. "Of course, I know about this fine citizen. I read the mental health journals, you know, and I have followed her political activities closely. I also know her personal history, and I want to say that she is, most probably, the finest example of what we attempt to create here in our women's facility. As Mrs. Packard advocates, we want our patients to learn to think in terms of improving society and not negating it. The dark land of Hades is not evil, but it does contain only the secrets of dead minds and isolated spirits. Nothing of value can come from retreating deep within oneself, ignoring the society around one, communicating only with the phantoms of illusion and dread."

Clara noticed that Mrs. Packard had brought out her full armaments. She held a rather ornate and collapsible ear trumpet against her right ear as Rooney spoke. It bothered Clara slightly that Liz hadn't used it when she was conversing with them earlier, but this was, obviously, a more important event.

"I am afraid I cannot accept your assessment of what the so-called lunatic community aspires toward, one way or another. I do know your classical analogy is a bit out of context. Hades raped and kidnapped Persephone, his mistress, as she was distracted by a symbol of her selfish, outer beauty, the Narcissus flower. Allow me to explain the myth contextually, just the way I explain it to asylum residents who are confused by their retreat from reality."

"By all means. Please do so," Dr. Rooney said. Clara noted a tone of slight sarcasm.

"Have you, by any chance, Dr. Rooney, ever attempted to go inside a patient's delusion, so to speak? In this method of conversation, you adhere to your patient's mental rules, not to your own nor society's rules. Is that not correct?"

Dr. Rooney was signing an admittance form, probably the same way he approved Bertha May's commitment, and he was distracted. When he finally looked up, he cocked his head to the side like a bulldog. "What was that? I am sorry, but this is the busiest time of year for us."

"That's fine. Your behavior answers my question. The way I approach mental health therapy is to attempt to be on an equal psychic footing with the ill person. You see, although Hades and his underworld can represent a retreat from reality, I prefer to tell my fellow voyager that she has been swept under because she must learn to accept death and the spirit world as a way to learn how to balance her inner world with the outer world. Both worlds are needed for health, but none is more important than the other. Persephone, in fact, is able to convince Hades that a heavenly place was necessary in his dark world, so he created the Elysium paradise for her, which later became the basis for the Bible's Garden of Eden." Mrs. Packard smiled.

"Liz, would you happen to be playing Demeter, Persephone's mother, and the Goddess of Nature, in this story?" Clara asked, also smiling. The attorney believed she knew where Mrs. Packard was going, so she wanted to assist her.

"I play whomever seems to fit with the individual's inner world. Sometimes, I will have a woman who has retreated because she was raped by her father or by some other close family member. This woman will often abuse herself physically, until she realizes it was not her role as a sexual temptress which caused her guardian to molest her. No, it was a social problem that made this woman feel guilty about her own sexual urges. Daughters were taught to love their parents, and when that trust was violated, such as in the case of an incestuous rape, then the violated woman must escape the only way she knows how, inside her own mind."

"I completely understand. However, I must say, we really don't have the time nor staff to explore such deeply disturbing areas. We believe if the body is exercised, cleansed, and kept fit, then the mind will soon follow. There is no need for such a dangerous and peculiar methodology. Sexuality is for the family and the clergy to investigate." Rooney clicked his teeth. "Can we get to the gist of your visit? I have to see to my responsibilities. Dinner is being served, and I must make my rounds."

Clara realized it was time for her to draw the line in the sand. She took out the papers from her purse that officially notified the State of California about their petition to investigate the asylum for reasons of possible improper treatment of patients, unsuitable handling and distribution of drugs, and how residents are wrongly admitted and for what reasons they are admitted. Mrs. Packard had already signed on to be an official on Clara's committee, and Clara was going to explain to the superintendent what they were planning to do in the coming days.

"Mr. Rooney, we are here not only to address the recent handling of Polly Bedford and her confinement, we are also planning to convene a citizens' investigation committee, to evaluate your overall services and health care of all those admitted to these confines." Clara leaned over and handed the copy of the application to Rooney.

She knew the State had its own yearly quality control inspection, but those were usually held on the asylum's schedule, and no process of examination was conducted with any specific purpose in mind. It was strictly a sheet with a check-off list of possible violations. Also, various merchants and wealthy California investors would be paraded past the asylum residents, during what Clara believed to be a pre-arranged dog and pony show, in order to demonstrate to these possible donors just how efficient their system was. However, Clara and her team would be the first truly independent, nationally recognized group to visit these premises.

"I see. And what do you expect to find during your inquest, pray tell? We have been lauded by many different groups for our dynamic and kind treatment of the mentally ill. In fact, we have a medical group from Germany who will soon be studying our research into the hereditary aspects of *dementia praecox* and *mania a potu.*" Rooney leaned back in his chair and waved his hand backward toward a row of plaques and awards decorating the redwood walls.

"We want to live here while we work. In addition to Mrs. Packer, we will have five or perhaps six committee members. Do you have accommodations for us?" Clara stood up.

"Yes, we can put you in the first floor guest wing. I'm afraid you will have to live as our residents do. We have a large room with bunkbeds. Will that be sufficient to your needs?" Mr. Rooney also rose.

Mrs. Packard stood up and took the ear trumpet from her ear. "I shall need a larger bed, young man. At seventy-one, I am not as flexible as I used to be. Even my three years in an asylum did not prepare me for old age. If women can escape death during childbirth, they still must face the arthritis, rheumatism, hip dislocations and missing teeth of old age."

Clara and Laura got on either side of Mrs. Packard and escorted her out into the main admissions hall. Superintendent Rooney followed them.

"After dinner, I think I shall roam the wards to meet some of my neighbors," Mrs. Packard said, hitching up her dress. "It is at night when the restless manias come out to play, is not that the case, Doctor Rooney?"

"Why, yes. We have nurses on duty, however, so if anybody gets lost, we can get her safely back into bed. There are also the ghosts, however." Clara looked at the superintendent's face to see if he were smiling. He was not.

"Did you say ghosts?" Laura, the spiritual skeptic, thrust her forefinger into Clara's ribs.

"I did. You may think me an inflexibly scientific sort, but I am actually a great believer in the spirit world. Whenever one of my women dies, if she has not been cured, then I believe her spirit stays around our home until she can be released. Release comes when a new patient is cured. It is the great circle of mental health, is it not?" Dr. Rooney stepped out in front of them to lead them into the dining room.

Clara could smell the lamb and potatoes, and she was suddenly quite famished. Dinner and then bed sounded very comforting. She knew the relief would be short lived, as the curse may still be out there, and now there were these ghosts. At the very least, she would probably have to follow after Mrs. Packard just to keep her out of trouble. Clara might also be accosted by her daughter, Bertha May, but this was to be prevented, at all costs. It may be a long night after all.

Chapter 4: Adeline the Spy

Leland Stanford Mansion, California and Powell Streets, San Francisco, April 24, 1887.

As Adeline Quantrill walked up to the mansion, which was just a stone's throw from her friends' Queen Anne Victorian abode at One Nob Hill, she was thinking about having been chosen by Mrs. Foltz. It was Adeline's firmest belief that if she were to stand any chance at marrying the attorney's son, Samuel, she would have to show that she could perform well on her first solo mission.

The young psychic was especially concerned, in that her ability to navigate on her own was probably her weakest trait. She had no sense of direction. True. It was her intellectual ability to read minds and telepathically communicate that made her so important to Mrs. Foltz solving the spiritualist murders the year before. In addition, Adeline's autobiographic memory allowed her to access every waking moment of her entire life to remember everything that occurred. This case was giving her all the authority to make her own mistakes, completely alone.

The mansion's structure was more of a Greco-Italian version of an imaginary home somebody so wealthy would build. Whereas the Hopkins' mansion was painted gray, Mr. Stanford chose white. Instead of the Hopkins' tall, cylindrical columns that had the religious appearance of a cathedral, this home had the squat, non-sectarian, and rectangular shape of the Greek Parthenon.

As one of the "Big Four" railroad tycoons, Leland Stanford was not enamored of helping to showcase new artists the way Mary Hopkins was. He was concerned with business and the appearance of grandeur. As Adeline entered through the twenty-foot tall granite and marble Corinthian columns, supporting the front porch entrance, she was not surprised by the type of decorative memorabilia inside. When Adeline, in a low whisper, gave her name to the butler, an older gentleman dressed in formal tails, he nodded, and he escorted her across the redwood floor beneath the house's mammoth circular rotunda.

She asked the butler who had created the statues and paintings, and she was informed it was one man, a Mr. G. G. Garibaldi, who had carte blanche when he furnished the mansion. The ceiling of the grand dome was divided into eight large panels. As she looked up, following the butler's pointed index finger, she was informed that each panel had a picture, four of which were figured with noble allegorical groups of female figures representing the four quarters of the globe. The other four panels were finished with emblematic figures personifying "Fine Arts," "Mechanics," "Agriculture" and "Literature."

As the butler led Adeline into the Library on the ground floor, she recognized the grand figure of Mr. Stanford almost immediately. He was standing in his black suit, vest and cravat tie, and he was looking down at a book opened on the long mahogany table. Hundreds of other volumes looked down upon its sibling from their cases along all four walls. Stanford was leaning on a black cane with an ivory handle, amongst the green and gold chairs, and Adeline noted with interest that Mr. Stanford's legs trembled uncontrollably, beneath his wide girth, as he leaned over to read the text. At sixty-three, his beard hair was almost all white under the gas chandeliers, although he still had streaks of black on top, and in his thick, furrowed eyebrows.

Leland Stanford, Adeline's prospective employer, was speaking to another man, also in a business suit, who was seated. This man, however, was clean shaven, and he wore a bowed tie. The hair around his mostly bald head was gray, and his white, mutton chop sideburns extended below his ears. His upper lip, Adeline noticed, came to a point, giving him a pouty expression. She also noted, with some amount of pleasure, that she could receive his thoughts.

Although she could not read the minds of many people, there were those rare individuals who seemed to have a supernatural affinity for her telepathic reception. One such person was Osiris Buddha Randolph, the twelve-year-old son of the spiritualist, Dr. Paschal Beverly Randolph. The year before, her communication with the boy led to saving Mrs. Foltz and her daughter, Trella Evelyn, from the villain at the Sarah Winchester house in San Jose.

This man was thinking, *I hope he finishes soon. I must make my appointment at Berkeley before noon.* However, when Adeline attempted to transmit her own thoughts to this gentleman, he would not answer. She had experienced this before with others, but not very often. She had known only two people who were only transmitters and not both transmitters and receivers. Either this man was refusing to allow her to know he was also a telepath, or he was afraid to send because Mr. Stanford was in the room.

"After I read your book, I knew you should be the person to formulate my science and psychology departments," Mr. Stanford was saying. "Shortly after we buried my son, I had an apparition of his countenance appear to me during sleep. I was afraid that I would not be able to bequeath anything now that I was bereft of an heir. I was even wondering if I should live anymore. My son spoke to me that night, Mr. Galton, and he said, 'Father, you can give to all of humanity in remembrance of me.' And, that's why you're here, good sir. You can assist me in building the largest university in the world devoted to the betterment of mankind."

If I had known you were a Spiritualist, I would not have come. Adeline heard Mr. Galton's thoughts. When he turned toward her and stared, she believed he might have finally recognized she was listening in to what he was thinking. She then realized that Mr. Galton was actually thinking about Mr. Stanford.

Mr. Galton was moved to reply, "My wife, Louisa, and I were never able to conceive. This is an important part of the over-population problem we face. While the inferior races and the degraded poor are having millions of offspring, we, who have been evolving and producing the superior offspring, are not generating

46

our children fast enough to compensate for the inevitable onrush of the barbarian stock."

"Excuse me, sir. May I intrude? This is Miss Adeline Quantrill. She has come to audition for the laboratory assistant position you need for Mr. Galton."

Both men turned toward Adeline, and she thought she smiled at them. However, when she saw her reflection on the wall mirror behind Mr. Stanford, the disfiguration of lips beneath her nose resembled that of a gorilla or chimpanzee attempting to mimic the grin of her betters.

"Thank you, Frederick. You may go." Leland Stanford chose that moment to swivel his rather portly back side down into one of the library chairs. The expiration of breath, as he fell into a seated position, was then followed by an expiration of stomach gas. The latter sound was so loud as to frighten a lounging Persian cat from the table.

Adeline, at nineteen, could not resist chuckling, as the feline scurried, slipping and sliding, from the library's confines, away from this creature with such great sounds erupting from it. Adeline thought momentarily of following the cat to safety.

Without any embarrassment, Mr. Stanford reached for a file on the table, took out its contents, and began his inquisition into her life.

"Young lady, Miss Quantrill, thank you for coming. This gentleman has come all the way from England, at my request, in order to work on a particular task of monumental importance. It is our immediate aim to take your experience and character into consideration, but please be aware that our questions are not meant to be an imposition upon your value to society. It's simply that we have a private agenda in mind. Is that clear?" Mr. Stanford looked over at her, and she was reminded of the way the judge and social welfare experts had looked at her after her parents were murdered on the train to San Francisco. Adeline wondered how much he already knew about her.

"I am honored to be here," she replied. "Your grand purpose must be important, and I can't help but wonder why you chose me as a candidate. After all, I have just begun my studies at Berkeley, and I have yet to declare my major study discipline." Adeline hoped her answer would be enough to extract the hidden reason behind their request to meet her.

"Very well. Since I am not the person who will be working with you, I am going to give Mr. Galton the opportunity to question you for his needs. Is that permissible, Miss Quantrill?" Mr. Stanford leaned forward and squinted at her.

"Of course. If I shall have the honored gentleman as my supervisor, I am eager to hear what he requires from an assistant." Adeline turned toward the Englishman, and she heard him thinking about her.

She is the only candidate with no parents. Good. That means she will not have any direct familial bonds to distract her from being objective. "Miss Quantrill, are you familiar with the two most important science books in the world, written by my cousin, Charles Darwin? *On the Origin of Species*, published in 1859, and *Descent of Man, and Selection in Relation to Sex,* published in 1871?"

Not only had Adeline read these books, she had also committed them to her prolific memory. Her autobiographic recall was pulling their images up on her inner brain screen as he was speaking the titles. She and Samuel had discussed the most controversial applications of what Mr. Darwin posited in their many arguments concerning the importance of biological inheritance in modern society.

"Yes, sir. I know those books quite well." Adeline replied.

"In point of fact, I was honored by having my own studies cited eleven times in his second book. Do you believe that breeding and natural selection form the building blocks for the evolution phenomenon, including the development of humankind and its resulting civilizations?" *This should open up her thought processes sufficiently for me to evaluate her abilities to reason on a higher level.*

"Although I respect Mr. Darwin's work, and I can completely agree with him as to his ideas concerning the methods of adaptation and survival that our natural world contains, when he extrapolates his theories into our own society, I am afraid I must begin to disagree." Adeline watched the face of the distinguished researcher and explorer. His manner was relaxed, and he smiled back at her. He was even keeping his thoughts private.

"Since you would be a close assistant, I am going to tell you a fact about myself that will allow you to understand how important Darwin's theories are to my own. When I was a bit older than you, and I was about to take my honors exams at Cambridge, the very thought of spending eight days and five and one-half hours of each day, writing about mathematics and statistical analysis, in order to prove my worth to my professors, was too much for my mind to process. As a result, I did not earn my doctorate, I withdrew from college, and so my credentials may not appear on paper to be sufficient." Mr. Galton looked over at Mr. Stanford and smiled.

Mr. Stanford struck the table with his clenched fist, and Adeline winced from the noise. "Balderdash! Give me a man who works with his hands and sets sail to travel the world to prove his theories correct. That is why your cousin chose your work over others."

"Please. I want you to look at a letter I wrote to my dear sister, Adèle." Mr. Galton took a letter from his vest pocket and handed it to Adeline. She read it to herself slowly:

"My Dear Adèle, I am 4 years old and I can read any English book. I can say all the Latin Substantives and Adjectives and active verbs besides 52 lines of Latin poetry. I can cast up any sum in addition and can multiply by 2, 3, 4, 5, 6, 7, 8, 9, 10, 11. I can also say the pence table. I read French a little and I know the clock.

FRANCIS GALTON,
Febuary 15, 1827"

Adeline returned the letter. "I am astounded, sir. You were obviously a child prodigy. Excepting the misspelling of the month, your epistle is perfect."

Mr. Galton folded the letter carefully and slid it back into his pocket. *Now I shall ask her the question which will prove her worth.* "My sister was an excellent and patient teacher. However, do you believe it was her skill as a teacher that allowed me to learn so quickly? Or, was my ability innate, a product of my family's excellent ancestry and long line of successful athletes, gun merchants, bankers, and academics?"

Adeline realized she had to respond in the way Mr. Galton required. She decided she would risk it all with her attempt. "My differences are not with your esteemed cousin's research and logic. His scientific examples of natural selection and species adaptation are impeccable. And, I do accept the fact that it was your excellent breeding and family's evolution that gave you your mental ability and strong character."

Her inquisitor nodded. "Yes, but what about your difference? I am curious. I believe your intelligence is superb, and you can show me how well you think from what you tell me now." *You had better not make a mistake at this point, or your chance at becoming my assistant will disappear.*

"My difference was voiced in the argument made by Mrs. Antoinette Blackwell in her book, *The Sexes Throughout Nature*. Mr. Darwin's theory of natural selection by females, in her opinion, was defrauding the advancement of womanhood." Adeline inhaled, believing it was best to quote a source who had credibility, even as a woman, in the dispute. She noted that the faces of these men were not irritated. Their expressions remained attentive and interested.

Therefore, she continued, "Darwin said that merely by choosing tools and weapons of superior quality, man had become superior to woman. I say, however, that choices first must be permitted by a society, and our society does not allow us women to make those same choices and learn those same trades that make men superior."

Mr. Stanford frowned for the first time. "Those choices, my dear lady, are often fraught with danger and possible death. What about inevitable war and conflict? Women are the keepers of the home and hearth, are they not?"

"Saint Joan of Arc, who was burned for heresy for her bravery, helped the French win the battle of Orleans during the Hundred Years War. Most recently, my dear sir, there were, by conservative estimates, over five hundred women who clandestinely took up arms during our Civil War."

Adeline was almost going to read off her photographic memory's list of the exact names of the women she knew who had fought in battles, but she refrained from doing so. Because of the reddened face of Leland Stanford, she believed it was time for her to soften her rhetoric.

She continued, using a technique she saw Mrs. Foltz use when arguing. She smiled, and then she made her voice into a lilting, sing-song refrain. "In effect, are not many women, in the best families, being kept like household pets? We cannot vote; we cannot make contracts; we cannot own property; we are children with adult bodies. We are a species Mr. Darwin ignores. Are we being given the same chances as men to prove our innate qualities? Perhaps, with the same educational and political opportunities for both males and females, our society would evolve twice as quickly as it is doing today."

Mr. Galton stared at her for several minutes, placing his right forefinger to his chin and holding onto his elbow with his other hand. His gaze was pecuniary but not malicious. Adeline did not hear him thinking negative thoughts about her. He finally sighed deeply and walked over to where Mr. Stanford was seated. He bent over and whispered into his ear for another two minutes.

At long last, Mr. Galton turned back toward her, and Adeline held her breath. This could mean her future. She needed to impress Mrs. Foltz, so as to win the heart of Samuel, and perhaps even be accepted into the hallowed world of male influence.

"One last question, Miss Quantrill," Mr. Galton said. "Do you enjoy working with identical twins?"

Adeline was dumbfounded. To what on earth could that question be in reference? "I must admit. I have never had the pleasure of seeing identical twins. However, I would most certainly find it intellectually stimulating and amusing to study or investigate such miracles of birth."

You will most certainly have your time filled with these twins. Mr. Galton puffed out his chest and looked over at Mr.

Stanford, who returned Galton's stern gaze and nodded. "When can you begin? I cannot promise to be with you more than one or two hours per day, but I can certainly get you started on your new work."

Adeline coughed into her fist. "I don't want to appear presumptuous, Mr. Galton, but what wage will I be earning for this work? Will it require the nursing care of children or babies? I would expect a bit higher wage if that were the case."

Indeed. You are most certainly an American capitalist. "I am prepared to pay you the sum of fifteen dollars per day, which will include room and board. Also, my twins are actually identical triplets, three each, of both genders, and they are eighteen and twenty years of age. The ladies are eighteen, the lads twenty." Galton's walk to the library entrance doors was, to Adeline, quite resolute. His stride, in fact, was almost a march cadence. He turned the gold handle, opened one of the doors wide, and shouted into the hallway.

"Roberts! I say, can you bring in the twins? We're ready."

What occurred next was to live in Adeline's dreams, in the form of vivid nightmares, for weeks following. There were six adults who entered the library, but it was their physical composition that sent a shiver down Adeline's spine. Two sets of the twins were conjoined. The males at the hip, the females at the chest and thorax. The other two identical siblings were normal. Adeline believed, however, that the term "normal" could hardly be accurate. Even if each three did not live together, the psychological pressures of being identical, combined with the physiological limitations of being fused together, must have been tremendously bothersome to all of them.

Even with their dragging feet, slumped-over torsos, and crab-like ambulation, these future laboratory subjects were quite handsome and alluring, in a uniquely macabre way. The conjoined men and women had exactly the same bodies and clothing as their siblings, and their faces were so exactly identical that Adeline kept scanning from one face to the other to see if there were even the slightest differences. No more exact replicas could have been created, even if they had been brought to life in some kind of successful Dr. Frankenstein laboratory experiment.

"These are the Falcone Triplets and the Johansen Triplets. Roger, Jerimiah and Claiborne were born in Edinburgh, Scotland in 1867, to Sir Robert and Emily Falcone. The Falcones come from a long line of nobility, extending back to the First Scottish War for Independence in the Thirteenth Century. The Falcone males fought with William Wallace in their attempt to seize power from King Edward the first. Each generation, the Falcones improved their status and wealth, with men who worked in Civil Engineering, fought for the King's military, explored scientific research at Cambridge, and managed four tobacco plantations in the New World, until the War for Independence by the United States, after which they sold their interests at a very good profit." Mr. Galton nodded to the lone Falcone, Claiborne, who stepped forward.

"Thank you, Mr. Galton. My name is Claiborne, and I am the eldest, at ten minutes. My brothers, I like to say, were so obnoxious in the birth canal about who should go next that they became fused together at the hip from the heat of their combined invective and fisticuff exchanges. However, we have all graduated from Cambridge with honors, and we hope to begin teaching there following our present work under our esteemed polymath and professor." Both Roger and Jerimiah applauded. Claiborne stepped back to stand beside them.

Claiborne, Adeline noted, unlike his two conjoined brothers, was tall and muscular, about five feet and ten inches of full manhood, with a pomaded black pompadour that glistened under the chandelier lamps. They had no facial hair, which was very appealing to Adeline, as her love, Samuel, also twenty, preferred shaving his face as well. Each young man had a most adorable curl, which snuck down at the upper-left corner of the forehead, like an added comma, as if to connect the grammatically perfect physiology of their hawk-like, amber eyes, with the matching facial accent of one coiling dimple in each triplet's cheek. They all wore light-brown cashmere frock coats, matching trousers, and vests that dangled gold watch fobs with chains.

These young women, on the other hand, were no

suffragettes. They had no sense of seriousness or purpose. Flittering about in their city finery, these three beauties knew they were attractive, and they knew how to use that temptation to its fullest extent. The satin frock with the large bustle was made uniquely to fit both bodies of the sisters who were fused together. Blonde, silky-smooth tresses curled over strong shoulders and down between six passionate globes of bounty.

Mr. Galton was not about to do the same introductory courtesy, and so he merely waved at the girls the way a child would wave at the caged tigers in a passing circus parade. "Trust me," he said, his pointy upper lip thrust forward. "these ladies are from the finest families and the noblest stock."

One of the sisters decided she would step forward to introduce them to the officious gathering. "We are honored to be part of this noble experiment for the betterment of civilization. My name is Deandra, and Susanne is one of the Thoracopagus duo, residing happily on the left, and Matilda is the artistic genius on the right. Her paintings are selling internationally. Susanne and I perform in a chamber ensemble in Stockholm. I play the piano; she, the violin. Matilda really pays no attention to us, as she paints while we play."

"All right now, pay attention please. This is Miss Quantrill. She has been awarded the pleasant task of being appointed your ward, tutor, and ombudsman. I expect that you will give her the utmost respect, as she is my direct representative when I am not present." Mr. Galton's voice rose at the end of the sentence in expectation.

"Yes, Mr. Galton!" The six answered in rehearsed union.

Mr. Stanford got up and addressed them. "I am afraid I must leave you all now. Congratulations on your new endeavor and best of fortunes building the roots of our new, progressive society!"

Not until Stanford had gone did Mr. Galton again begin to speak to them.

"We are not going to hide what we are doing from you. The instruction I shall give to Miss Quantrill tomorrow will also be given to you. I am of the belief that a society moves that much faster when it knows the ultimate purpose behind its labors. I must remark at the outset that I am very proud to have you all as important parts of this monumental study. I have been told by our benefactor, the great philanthropist, scholar, and world traveler, Leland Stanford, that we must move to the state asylum in Stockton to do this work. We shall have complete privacy, but I hope it's not an inconvenience to the newest member of our research group.

Adeline's pulse quickened. She had some previous experience with mental wards. When you are a girl who tells adults she can hear their thoughts, and then they realize that you do indeed know what they are thinking, the tables, as Jesus would say, begin to turn. They put you into a white room, with padded walls, and with one small hole in the giant door in front of you. Imaginary snakes and vermin also use that hole.

"No, sir. It would be no imposition. I am proud to be a part of your research, and I am very happy to meet all of these fine ladies and gentlemen. I will do my utmost to teach you all that I know about what it takes to advance in this society, and I will follow Mr. Galton's directions exactly, in the best interests of science." Adeline turned to face Mr. Galton, who was busy taking the thumb prints of the triplets. He took each one by his or her thumb and pressed it firmly down on individual cards laid out on the table in the center of the room. Adeline knew he had recently written a paper about his study concerning finger print marks. Mr. Galton believed that each print was completely unique and that it could conceivably be used as a means of identification for the police or other proper authorities.

You have the misconception that I cannot hear you. Say something. I will respond.

Adeline heard these words, and her blood turned icy. She reacted rather than pondered the consequences. *Thank you for being honest, Mr. Galton. However, I might never have believed you were a telepath in addition to being a polymath.*

He laughed. His voice was high-pitched and effeminate. Adeline wondered vaguely if he might even be capable of humor. She believed the home of Swift and Pope should have nobles, even noble scientists, who could appreciate a satirical jab or two, or three, or four.

Oh, Miss Quantrill. You shall enjoy your new appointment. I chose you exactly because you are a telepath. I also know you are far more talented than your lowly academic status would bely. Your mind is a literal box of history as it was lived. Yours is the most historically accurate mind of all. To me, your value is inestimable.

Mr. Galton turned to the six youths. "Off to bed with you! We must move tomorrow, and I want you all rested."

All six came to give Mr. Galton and Adeline a personal hug before retiring. When Claiborne came up to her, Adeline became a bit nervous. Again, her pulse quickened, but this time it was because she imagined her brain to be shrinking to the size of a pea, and the resultant pressure was driving her arteries insane.

"Good meeting with you, Miss Quantrill," Claiborne bent forward and whispered in her ear. "We are really Jews. Surname is Feldman. This man is insane. Get out while you can. I am staying here only to protect the others." Claiborne's gray eyes were glistening with emotion, and Adeline felt his chest heave, with a deep inhale, as he turned on his heels and left the room.

Chapter 5: The Five

The Women's Section, First Floor, Stockton State Insane Asylum, Morning, April 25, 1887.

Francis Galton had his projects organized as if he were spending his own money. The voyage to San Francisco had given him the time to arrange the stages of his experiments. He was also able to study the backgrounds of the five subjects that were being provided to him by Dr. Alfred Rooney. Francis understood that his reputation as a scientist was at stake, so he was prepared to proceed like a scientist.

Like his benefactors, Francis believed that the problems of minority races and hereditary genetics were growing exponentially in the United States. In order to provide the proof necessary to convince lawmakers that change was needed, Galton was given this chance at the Stockton State Asylum to do so. He knocked on the door of Rooney's office with a firm conviction. The Superintendent was waiting for him, and he answered the door almost immediately.

"Francis Galton! What a pleasure. We've been corresponding all these months, and now I have a chance to meet you in person. Quite an honor. Quite an honor indeed." Francis followed the taller man into his large office. He sat in the leather chair in front of Rooney's wide mahogany desk.

"Thank you, Alfred. I am pleased to finally meet you." Francis took the five files from his briefcase, leaned forward, and placed four of them on the top of the superintendent's desk.

Rooney pointed to the obligatory photo of Washington Bartlett, the current California governor, whose white-bearded face was smiling down at them from the wall behind his desk. "He's a

Jew, you know. This is what our so-called democracy allows. The insinuation into our midst of the race that killed Jesus."

Francis nodded and opened the file of the first woman chosen to become one of his research experiments. "I trust you have the five women domiciled in a secure location?"

"Of course. Do you mind if I call you Francis? I feel like I know you already." Rooney smiled.

"I don't mind at all. This appears to be the informal way you California chaps do business." Francis looked down at the record in his hands. "I want to go over these five women and their backgrounds. Then, if possible, I would like you to introduce them to me."

"Of course, Francis. They are interred on the second floor, in a locked suite, with five beds and a separate washroom. They do not mingle with the wealthy patients or with any other member of my staff other than me." Rooney leaned forward in his chair. "Are those the files I sent you?"

"Yes, they are. As you've already broached the topic of race, let's discuss our first subject, Miss Sidney Reyes. I believe her family and friends call her Kitty?" Francis looked down at the photo of the young woman. She was wearing the navy blue uniform of the asylum, with her initial "SR" stitched on her left shoulder. She had the inferior expression of her Filipina-Asian ancestry: slanted eyes, oval face, weak chin, and wide nose. Her black, stringy hair was parted down the middle, and she was seated on her chair with her legs apart, like a man, and her hands on her knees.

"Reyes. Of course. They all receive Spanish surnames since Spain's occupation. She came alone to the United States in 1885, and arrived in San Francisco. Her parents sent her away because they were members of the movement for independence, and they were afraid she would be hunted down. When she found out her parents were executed in Manila, for following the novelist and rebel, José Rizal, she became withdrawn and secluded. She has retained the rebellious streak of her parents and her kind, and yet her mental illness also contains a proclivity for retreating into a private, fantasy world, known only to her."

Francis picked the photo up and looked at the notes beneath it, which he had made about this woman. "And yet, it says you committed her for neurasthenia. It was love sickness that placed her here, and you are aware that this type of perverted amorousness makes her my candidate."

"Yes, Francis. I am well aware. She was in love with another female." Rooney frowned. "Not only was she disobeying the laws of nature, she was also a moral degenerate."

"This type of illness can be traced to her heritage. The Asiatic mind is filled with immoral fantasies, and their genetics make them prime candidates for my experiments. I am anxious to meet her." Francis closed the folder on Miss Reyes and picked up the second folder from the desk.

"I understand. California has become, as in many other states, a refuge for the Asian, especially from China. They were supposed to go back to China when they worked on our railroads, but they decided to stay. That's why we passed the federal law against further immigration of these pagans. They were trying to take the jobs of white Americans, but many of them go insane, so we have to house them." Dr. Rooney coughed into his fist. "Please, continue, Francis."

"This woman has auburn hair, and her name is Angela Thoma. She is married, and her family calls her Angie, or Ang. We have reason to believe her hysterical activities are hereditary by nature, as the entire family has been known to follow her into deserted battle fields, graveyards, and other insane asylums looking for ghosts. The alienist, a Dr. Forbes of San Jose, said she was committed when it was determined she could not have children. That's when she began to go out alone to trespass and to put herself at risk of arrest and even death. She insists she has the ability to speak with the dead, and this is why she hunts for their spirits, even if she must break into such private domiciles to do so."

Dr. Rooney struck his fist on the desk top. "Quite right! We know that these types of hysterics are often faking it in order to gain sympathy and to get out of household work. The hysteria is frequently caused by the reproductive problems they have. Quite often, as you may know, they are brought out of their delusion by bringing them to orgasm and by using techniques such as cold-water showers, interruption of their breathing, shaving their heads, and disgracing them in front of their family members. In this case, the husband is as delusional as the wife. He insists she can communicate with ghosts, as he has seen her do it."

Francis closed the folder. "I want to determine how such a physically attractive woman, in her thirties, can become such a mentally unstable patient. Once I can determine the actual source of her hereditary disease, we can perhaps provide a cure for all such hysterical cases."

Francis picked up the third folder from Dr. Rooney's desk.

"This woman. This Melissa Kay Wilkinson. She is the only criminal lunatic of our five, is she not?" The Englishman held up her photo.

"Correct. She was adjudicated insane by Judge Samuel Crawford of San Francisco in 1885. We moved her to Stockton this year as you requested."

Francis placed the photo down on the desk and picked up the notes on the woman inside the folder. "I believe her type of murderess, quite possibly, can be traced to a genetic cause. She was found inside her mansion on Nob Hill, wandering the luxurious halls, still wearing the same wedding dress, but it was bloodied and in tatters. She was quite hysterical and mute. Although her family is intelligent, with artists and poets among its members, they all have eccentricities that are against the norm. Our young lady, Pepper, as she's called, stabbed her newlywed husband, Jeremy, on their wedding night. When asked why she had done this, she replied that he had refused to allow her to dip her food into the condiments of tomato ketchup and salad dressings."

Dr. Rooney chuckled. "Yes. That's our Pepper, all right. As you can imagine, she is not allowed near any object that can be dangerous to her or to the other patients."

"And yet, her gaze is quite penetrating, and it says she is a social chameleon. She loves to imitate the postures and affectations of whomever she's with. She writes long, anti-patriarchal diatribes with the finger paint supplies you provide to her, and she's quite sociable for being a hysterical mute."

Francis closed the folder. "If we can isolate the cause of her obsessions and get her to speak, I believe we may then trace the hereditary problem to its root cause."

"I admire your ambition on this case, Francis. I assume you have special tools with which you'll be working to do this?" A knock sounded on the office door. "Come in!" Dr. Rooney shouted.

The door opened, and Mrs. Betterman, the baker, tentatively stuck her head inside the doorway. "Dr. Rooney? Sorry to disturb. But that committee group from San Francisco is here again. Mrs. Foltz, the attorney, wants to know where they would be staying."

"Put them in the dining room until I'm finished here." Dr. Rooney brushed her away with his hand. "Such a bother! Can't you see we're busy?"

"Yes sir! I shall do so immediately." Mrs. Betterman, her face flushed, turned around, and closed the door behind her.

"Committee? What is that?" Francis inquired.

Dr. Rooney scowled. "We have a young patient, a Miss Polly Bedford, twelve years of age. She attacked another youngster, and because this Bedford child was committed by her quite wealthy parents, the newspapers follow her goings-on quite regularly. Some say she was witness to the murder of a ten-year-old girl at her parent's mansion. Others say she may have actually committed the act itself and then gone mad. This committee, as a result, is here to investigate our entire facility."

"And, this Foltz woman. Who is she, and who are these committee members?" Francis took up a pen and was ready to jot notes on one of the folders.

"Don't fret. I will not allow them to access any of our research areas. They will be restricted to the patients' quarters, the dining room, and my office. Mrs. Foltz has assembled this group, and I will be learning their full identities after we finish here. I will keep you completely informed, you can be certain."

Francis picked up another folder and opened it. "Indeed. We need to maintain the strictest secrecy in these matters, Alfred. It's a matter of life and death."

"We understand the stakes. My reputation is also on the line. Who do you have in that folder?" Dr. Rooney took out a cigar from his waistcoat pocket and offered it to Francis. When the Englishman refused, Rooney lit it with a flint lighter on his desk and puffed leisurely.

Francis read his notes on the fourth patient. "A most interesting woman. She has a delusional identity, among other problems. Her Christian name is Katherine Sue Yantis, but she believes she is Annie Oakley, the famous sharpshooter. I believe the actual Mrs. Oakley is now touring with the Buffalo Bill Wild West Show at the present moment. Mrs. Yantis claims this other woman is a fraud. They are both from Cincinnati, but Mrs. Yantis came west to seek fortune with her husband during the Gold Rush."

Dr. Rooney blew a smoke ring. "Yes, I knew she would be a good candidate for your experiments. This woman was certified as a modern witch, after she claimed to be able to change cats into women who would do her bidding. Her family also made macabre mementos from the hair and fingernails of known murderers, which she inserted into lockets and watches and sold at their hangings. They also put cremated ashes of pets and loved ones inside antique vases, statuary, and other artistic pieces. Several noted industrialists have done business with her and her family."

Francis smiled. "She is an obvious genetic freak with delusions of grandeur. I have just the remedy for her type, and if it proves to work, then we shall have evidence that witchcraft can be conquered with modern science."

Dr. Rooney laughed. "If you can simply rectify the delusions, it would cure over one hundred women presently inside our asylum. We can then work on the Congress of the United States."

"I agree. Once Eugenics has been recognized for what it causes in our general population, the government will pay attention. This Yantis woman is quite spirited and attractive to the eye. She should make a great story for your newspapers once I've cured her." Francis closed the folder and picked up the final one from Dr.

Rooney's desk.

"This is our youngest patient of the five. Miss Jessica Adkins. At the age of fourteen, she witnessed her best friend, Sarah, being murdered. She became a vicious and beautiful demon, refusing to go to school, to become socialized, or to learn the proper behavior of a young lady. Today, she believes that we are all figments of her personal dream." Dr. Rooney stubbed out his cigar in an ashtray.

Francis chuckled. "I see. I have had that perception myself, from time to time. I can understand her wanting to believe she is the center of existence. Our entire social realm is an attempt to frustrate that concept. As a lunatic, this young woman has become traumatized by the act of murder. As a result, she is protecting her own mind by believing she is, in fact, projecting all of what she observes, and that we should appreciate her for that act of kindness, if you will."

"I have never thought of it in just that manner, but yes, I can see what you mean." Dr. Rooney splayed his hands together, thrusting the intertwined fingers and palms forward, until they made an audible cracking sound. "What are your plans for Miss Adkins?"

"She is most important to my entire experiment in that I believe she will be able to unravel the puzzle that is Miss Polly Bedford, the entitled patient of whom we both understand to be witness to the murder which took place on Nob Hill. That murder, in point of fact, is the linchpin in the rebellion against my philosophy of Eugenics. The wealthy race of Caucasians, upon which most of the world's civilizations rest, cannot become victims of such atrocities!"

"Yes, Francis, but how can you stop such acts of rebellious murder? Certainly, an insane person is behind this murder." Dr. Rooney leaned forward, expecting a more focused response.

"The experiments I shall perform on these five women will give us the answer. As it was stated in Shakespeare's *Hamlet*. When the young prince sees the ghost of his dead father, the King, he says, 'And therefore as a stranger give it welcome. There are more things in heaven and earth, Horatio, than are dreamt of in your philosophy.'

We must be open to the magic this youngest and strangest of the five brings to us. She may be the key to communicating with lunatics everywhere."

***

Clara wired her son, Samuel, to tell him to take Dr. Andrew McFarland and his granddaughter, Anne, out to the Stockton asylum. He was to use one of the buggies from Mrs. Hopkins' stable on Nob Hill, and meet them at the train station in Stockton at three in the afternoon the following day. In the meantime, Clara was going to speak with the committee members who had joined them to meet with Dr. Rooney when he completed his business conference with an unknown visitor. The kindly baker, Mrs. Betterman, had escorted them into the patients' dining room on the first floor.

The members of the investigation committee had dwindled fast. Three of them, in fact, did not want to journey out to the asylum, giving a variety of excuses as to why they did not want to participate. Captain Lees said his judge was busy with a court trial, Ah Toy's labor representative mentioned something about "evil spirits," and her daughter, Trella Evelyn's favorite professor told her his reputation as a scholar could be held in question if he were to become involved with what he had termed the "insane academy." Trella told Clara that her esteem for this professor had consequently lessened because of his rebuff.

There were now six on Clara's committee, including the two arriving the next day. Laura Gordon would also be participating, as an attorney for the Cotton family. As she sat at the head of the physician's dining table at the front of the dining room, Clara nodded to each of her fellow investigators. Ah Toy sat on her left, and she was talking to Mrs. Packard, who was in the chair beside her friend. Captain Lees was to Clara's right, and Laura sat next to him.

"May I have your attention? I want to discuss our method of inspection before Superintendent Rooney appears." When they all turned to look at her, Clara continued. "Governor Bartlett has signed the authorization papers, which now give us authority to inspect the

64

premises, interview staff, and talk to patients. However, and this is a rather great exception, if you ask me. We cannot visit, under any circumstances, the second floor rooms where the wealthy patients reside. Bartlett has always been a protector of the upper classes, as we know from our experiences with him as Mayor of San Francisco. I believe we can use subterfuge to enter these quarters, as I have been informed that Adeline Quantrill, my son's friend, is now working inside the asylum on the second floor."

"Do you know what she's working on?" Ah Toy held her pencil above her pad, ready to jot down notes.

"No. It seems to be a top-secret endeavor. Since we have only three days ourselves to complete our inquiry, we shall have to wait to speak with Adeline following her duties upstairs." Clara cleared her throat. "Did you all sleep well last night in your new accommodations?"

Mrs. Packard, who held her hearing aid, spoke up. "I visited with a few wandering patients last night. They seemed tranquil after I told them of my own experiences in Illinois, and I was able to tuck them into bed. However, I did not see any of the ghosts. Thank goodness. If I had, then I might have considered becoming a resident myself."

They all laughed.

"Our method should be to discover how this asylum conducts its own subterfuge. The theories we've established will mean fewer persons to conduct searches, and yet we still have two important people in our group who can help us. Mrs. Packard, of course, will be able to interview patients, and Dr. McFarland and his granddaughter can investigate the use of tranquilizers and other drugs on the site."

"Don't forget that we still have your daughter Bertha here," Ah Toy pointed out.

"I certainly have not forgotten our implants, and that includes our psychic and mind reader, Adeline Quantrill. Our fishing expedition shall be conducted with a net that can gradually surround all the suspects at once, slowly tightening its grip until the guilty are aroused from their evil grottoes and attempt to escape from our confines." Clara took out a sheet of paper and scanned it with her forefinger. Her brow furrowed. "This is a list of our most possible suspects at this point. If you have other suggestions, please let me know. We can always add or subtract to it."

"Shall we be pursuing only the hunt for the murderer? Or, if warranted, will we be searching for bigger sharks, swimming in deeper waters, who may have ordered such a crime?" Isaiah Lees sat up straight in his chair and twisted his mustache. "My weaponry will always be at the ready to protect any of you who may get into danger."

"Polly Bedford is still a suspect in the murder of Winnie Cotton. She was the only person present in the house. What we learned from Bertha was that Polly was perhaps too drugged by Dr. Rooney to have a clear memory of the killer. That brings us to our second suspect, Dr. Rooney. He wanted to be personally involved in this investigation, to the point of making certain the Cotton family was represented by counsel."

Laura Gordon smiled. "And I am still in that employment," she said.

"Not a problem. We are also investigating with the best interests of the Cottons in mind. However, I am afraid, dear Laura, that your clients are our suspects three and four." Clara frowned. "Unless you can provide them with a proper alibi."

Laura returned the scowl. "There are no charges as yet, my dear. Be assured that if you do provide such warrants, I shall protect them."

"Finally, we cannot rule out Leland Stanford." Clara noticed the silence and the human question marks on their faces. "I told you I believe this entire plot could entail a culprit from the highest levels of society. It cannot be mere coincidence that the murder was committed on one of the most distinguished families in San Francisco. We must always be on the hunt for connections that tie us into the upper classes."

Elizabeth Packard raised her hand, and Clara nodded at her. "We discovered three such connections during our investigations of different asylums. One was indeed related to the murder of a patient, and the two others were drug overdoses prompted by illegal sales to the wealthy clientele, who had become addicted. The murderer was the superintendent, and I applaud your listing of Dr. Rooney. He was on my personal list of suspects also."

Clara looked down at her paper. "That brings me to another five suspects who were not calculated earlier."

"Five suspects? What in blazes?" Captain Lees stood up next to Clara and took hold of her arm. "What do you mean, Clara?"

"While Mrs. Packard was roaming the wards and causing a distraction, I was also roaming to a rendezvous with my future daughter-in-law, Adeline. She has informed me that her employment has been delegated from Leland Stanford to one Francis Galton."

"Galton? Isn't he the British cousin of Charles Darwin?" Trella Evelyn asked. "We've been studying them both in Biology. He has rather strange theories about heredity, does he not?"

"Indeed, his does, daughter. He also has five residents housed in this asylum, who shall be his personal laboratory test subjects. One is a convicted murderess, and the other four are also quite insane in their own right. Not only does this Galton want to prove something here, he also may want to establish links to identical triplets being capable of insane activities."

"Triplets? How so?" Ah Toy asked.

"Actually, they are not patients here. He brought them from his world travels to this place. For some unknown reason, he wants to prove something, and I do not rule out possible mind control for murderous intentions." Clara heard the door at the end of the dining hall open. When Superintendent Alfred Rooney entered, her pulse quickened, and she sat down, pulling Isaiah down with her.

"Ladies, and gentleman! So glad you have arrived. I have some news of my own to share," Dr. Rooney exclaimed, as he strode confidently toward them, his shiny leather dress shoes clicking on the newly polished tiles of the doctors' dining enclave. "After I tell you, I shall have someone escort you to your new room, as I must assist Francis Galton with his research."

Chapter 6: Sex, Mayhem and Squalor

The Women's Section, Second Floor, Stockton State Insane Asylum, Morning, April 26, 1887.

Sidney

None of these other women was her friend. Sidney "Kitty" Reyes was alone and hungry when they picked her off the street in downtown San Francisco. She did not know where she was, and she had lost the love of her life, Maria, a former slave who had come to town to work for Mary Ellen Pleasant, the "voodoo queen." When they discovered from Maria that Sidney was in love with her, in a very physical way, the young Filipina woman was chosen to become one of the lunatic subjects to be studied by a famous scientist from England, Francis Galton.

One of those nurses who frowned at her whenever she had to provide Sidney with new linen, or bathe her, take her for exercise, or administer ordered treatments, unlocked the door and entered. "Reyes. You're to come with me."

Sidney followed the short and stoutly swaggering older woman. It was the first time out of that room, and Sidney's black eyes observed every board in the floor, color on the wall, and other patients, who were wandering the upstairs. The Filipina could smell the noxious odors of French perfume and talcum powder wafting from these well-dressed women, and many were dancing alone, twirling their skirts, swirling in a circle, their diaphragms undulating their bosoms like the bellows keeping the fires lit in a house of ill repute. She could hear the sounds of freedom in the steps of these wealthy women, as they would never be hungry, on the move over rugged terrain, or cast their eyes frantically, wondering if they would be murdered and raped or forced to sell the last commodity known to be a good woman's product: her flesh and intimate talents.

"Here it is, number 75. Dr. Rooney and Mister Galton are in here, and I want you to understand your place. You hear me?"

Sidney nodded obliquely to the nurse, wondering to herself if she should curtsy or spit in their faces. When she passed into the room, she inhaled deeply, and she did what her mother in the Philippines always told her to do, "Prepare for the worst, expect the best, and you won't be disappointed."

"Aha, Miss Reyes! I see you've come at last." The old man with the grizzled gray lambchop sideburns and an old owl's penetrating gaze, rushed at her, arms extended. She darted away from him, twirling her entire torso so her right shoulder grazed his expensive blue waistcoat. She had done this, many times, to get away from drunken bounders in the streets, who poured out of the taverns by the dozens, looking for the restorative power of a receptive woman.

"Write that down, Dr. Rooney. Her physical proclivity is against the aggressive male form. It may be about the father, or the authority figure, and we shall certainly find out! Get her prepared. I want to begin immediately. I shall retrieve the Johansen ladies." The older man left the room.

The superintendent sat her down in a chair beside the window. He pulled up another chair, sat down, took hold of her hands, and stared at her. Sidney recoiled within herself, afraid of this man, but he slapped her face, and his palm caught her left ear. She slowly turned toward him, ear ringing, furrowing her brow, trying to remember the voodoo curse Maria had taught her, so she could inject it between this old man's rheumy eyes.

"You are very fortunate to be here, Sidney. Why, you might even become a woman who is talked about in research journals and at meetings of insane asylum leaders from around the world. We are going to attempt to discover the source of your abominable sickness. Have you always lusted after other females? Even back in the Philippines? I have read that in that island nation your kind are locked away forever inside Spanish prisons. Aren't you happy to be in the United States, where we attempt to cure you?"

Sidney now wanted to spit in Dr. Rooney's face. Instead, because she had learned how to survive in this nation by pretending to be submissive, she curled her lips into a possum-like smile. "I know my thoughts are sinful, Doctor. My mind is my enemy, and I am very happy to be under your care. What will he be doing to me?"

It was Dr. Rooney's turn to smile. She believed his smile was even more pretentious than hers. "Good. I am not aware of what Mr. Galton is going to try. You may rest assured, however, that it is in your best interest and in the best interest of the future of mankind."

The door opened once more, and into the room, walking sideways like a crab, Sidney watched the two, identically beautiful and blonde young women enter, attached together at their chests and throats. Their fine silk dresses, with scarlet petticoats, violet bustle and trim, belied their tiny, shuffling feet and the absurd connection of bone, sinew and flesh, which forced them into a sisterly union of a most uncommon and macabre sort.

Francis Galton, the man Sidney already feared, entered behind them, gazing upon these freaks of nature like a proud father. "Matilda and Susanne Johansen, from Sweden. Matilda, on the right, is an artist of the finest caliber. Susanne, on the left, has given concerts to King Oscar II of Sweden. Ladies, this is Miss Sidney Reyes of the Spanish kingdom of the Philippines."

Sidney stared at these two women. Their faces were identical, and each head, although the same shape and size, seemed to exist in different worlds. Matilda was gazing into space, her ruby lips pursed, her brow furrowed in concentration. The one he called Susanne, on the other hand, was watching Sidney like a hawk, her eyes wandering, most obtrusively yet fetchingly, up and down her body. It was Susanne who spoke.

"Miss Reyes. We are charmed, I'm sure."

"We shall now leave you ladies to your own devices. We want you to become acquainted. You will not be disturbed, as it is most important that you learn all about each other. The fragile mind of Miss Reyes can be affected very easily, and I want you twins to behave. You are the ones who are world travelers and sophisticates. Remember your *noblesse oblige*. Good morning to you, ladies. I shall return at noon to see how you've gotten on together."

Sidney's breathing quickened when the two men existed and closed the door. It was locked, and she was together with two women whom she did not know, but whose beauty, sophistication and physical abnormality attracted her in a unique way.

"My sister is the one who loves her own kind." Matilda spoke for the first time.

Sidney thought her voice was without sentiment. She was speaking as if she had done this, quite often, before.

Matilda continued, "I have learned to meditate from a Rabbi's son in Budapest. As you two women exchange your familiarity, I shall be focusing within, into my dream world, preparing my next work of art."

With those words, Matilda closed her eyes, began to breathe deeply and regularly, a slight smile hovering upon her lips.

Sidney stood up, walked slowly over the creaking wooden planks, to stand next to the identical twins. The bold stare from Susanne made Sidney's hair follicles prickle and tickle upon her olive skin.

"We can also be one, my lovely young maiden," Susanne said, reaching out with her alabaster right arm, with the delicate, bejeweled ring on her heart finger and the diamond bracelet encircling her thin wrist.

As Sidney pressed her lips to the top of Susanne's soft hand, she felt a joy enter her body that she had never experienced before. Her life of poverty, even the momentary dalliance with Maria, disappeared in a puff of exquisite perfume from between the white globes of this female monument to unique loveliness. Passion rose inside Sidney like the dawning of the rising full moon upon a lake filled with water lilies. She now wanted, more than anything else in the world, to touch her lips upon this beautiful woman's neck, and then, most slowly, and most lovingly, move down to enter the dominion of Sapho, in an expression of undying and forbidden love.

Angela

Angie plunged deep inside herself whenever she talked to the dead. Contact had to take place in the exact center of the white-hot reality that was non-being. Zen meditation was what it was. The way her Uncle Dill said it was. He had studied Zen under a master in Kyoto, Japan. True Zen, he told her, reaches the smooth path between the living and the dead. The spirits of these magical beings came floating above you, and you were able to snatch them out of the air. The catch, however, as Angela Thoma discovered, was that one had to be in a special place, where the dead's spirit essence was still trying to participate with the living.

Pulsations and hunger were the physical manifestations of Angie's manner of necromancy affinity. The pulsing took place in her erogenous zones. The small of her back, just above the spreading meadowlands of her passionate zones below; her lips, spread wide for the darting tongue of any human sexual spirit; her breasts, rising up, like two peaks of firm, silk-adorned dunes, decorated at the tops with pink buttons of dimpled delight. Her mouth would begin to salivate, setting off the oral and nasal battle between her taste buds and her odorous follicles, joining together with the delicate softness on the underside of her wrists, her neck, her belly, and her womb. The voices came to her, only when she was deep inside herself, and it was like standing on the edge of the Grand Canyon and jumping down into its stupefying beauty, without having to die in the flesh.

Instead, you melted into the mountains, the rivers, and the forests, like the natives, and you began to talk with the anxious ancestors.

"Thoma! Get your rump over here. I am taking you to meet somebody." The tall nurse, who, to Angie, resembled a puffy-headed crane, standing on one leg, had her right arm outstretched toward her. Angie shook her long auburn hair, and looked furtively at each of the other four women, as if she needed their permission to leave. She stood up from her bed, wrapped her arms tightly around her shoulders, and walked delicately toward the nurse, who was now standing just outside the doorway.

"Speed it up, Missy. I have things to do. You walk like you're inside a molasses vat." The nurse held the door and drummed her right hand's fingers upon the door-frame. When Angie finally passed her, and stood out in the hallway, the nurse slammed the thick door shut and locked it with a key she had hanging on a shoelace around her neck.

Angela had lost her way since her family decided to admit her to the asylum. They found her locked inside the remains of an old mansion down in the Bowery, on the Barbary Coast. The New Orleans-style building was owned by a French pirate, and it became deserted, after he was arrested and hanged on Russian Hill for shooting a gold miner in a game of poker.

She was called there by this pirate's spirit, she told her husband, Allan, when he found her there, and he drafted the commitment papers that same day. Even though Allan had believed she could communicate with the dead, when she was making money from her efforts as a medium, she was then no longer doing her motherly and household duties, so he believed she needed the repose and treatment. The rest of her family agreed, even though her youngest daughter, Camille, believed her mother could, indeed, talk to ghosts, and the family had to pull her off Angie's skirts when they took her away to the Stockton facility. Dr. Rooney, after seeing what her mental problems were, decided she was perfect for Francis Galton's research project.

"Go inside. She's waiting for you." The crane nurse opened the door with another key from around her neck. As Angie walked inside, with her arms still wrapped over her shoulders, her body's waist became a magnet, and she gasped when her feet felt frozen in place.

After the nurse closed and locked the door, Angela experienced a strange sensation. It was a gravitational pull that centered within her loins. She could not move, no matter how hard she tried. As the pulling became stronger, her entire body was shuffled along on the floor, without Angie taking one step of her own. It was if she were a spirit that no longer needed its body for locomotion.

"Angela, don't be frightened. I understand you." The young woman now holding onto both her shaking hands, was speaking, and yet Angie could not hear her. Her full concentration was upon a voice vibrating within her stomach, traveling up to her lungs, and then circling into her esophagus and into her ear canals. It was an eardrum-splitting shout that filled Angie with a terror she had never felt before, during all her years of searching out abandoned houses, and probing inside haunted buildings.

I died here, and now I am being called to murder another one. You must tell them to remove these strangers from the asylum! Unless I am free to roam, without intrusion from outsiders, there will be hell to pay!

When the sound became too much to bear, as it was so loud and so nauseating to her body, Angie crumpled over into the strange woman's arms and breathed into her ear in a panicked whisper, "You must leave here. You and whomever else are here from outside. Unless you go at once, there will be a murder committed!"

Katherine

Before the door to Katherine Sue Yantis' new reality opened, she was thinking about how to escape this prison of mental defectives in order to return to her family and to her employment with the Buffalo Bill Wild West Show. Her trigger finger was itching, and she smiled at the prospect of blasting her way out, watching all the rich women on the second-floor run, screaming for cover, the frilly petticoats getting soiled as they fell, their thick make-up running like a desert flash flood of tears. Or, she could turn any one of her psychotic roommates into cats, who could then infiltrate this hell hole and get the keys. There were so many possibilities when one was a witch.

Katherine knew, when the door opened, she was going to be taken to a place where she could be understood. The knob was turning, as the key was inserted, and she watched it swing open. The woman standing in the doorway was not a nurse, however. She did not wear the white dress and frilly cap. Instead, her look was cosmopolitan and well mannered. Her full-length dress had a stylish bustle, and it was orange, with black buttons down the front, and a matching hat that was shaped like a stove pipe but with a small bouquet of white flowers in the band. The silver cape she wore looked as if it were from some Eastern European court, with spots on its fur-lined insides and edges, as if the Czarina herself had ordered it.

This woman, as expected, sauntered directly over to Katherine, her gaze only vaguely taking in her compatriots. When she stood before her, Katherine could smell the expensive odor of her perfume. Her cheeks were rouged lightly, and her lips were puffy and scarlet. Her forehead was wide, and her ears were delicate, with passionate lobes and angelic, serenely blue eyes.

"Mrs. Oakley? I am here to invite you to a meeting with his royal majesty, the King of Sweden. He has heard of your skill as a markswoman and the magical prestidigitation you possess. Oscar the Second is going to be here in a fortnight. Can you accept his invitation to rendezvous under these rather squalid conditions?"

"And, who are you?" Katherine asked, sizing this lady up for a possible shape-shift into an orange tabby.

"I am the King's foreign secretary. Madeline Olsen. In Sweden, women are not as subservient to male domination as you are in these States. I have the authority to arrange such meetings, you can be assured. Here. Look at my passport."

With her right hand, Miss Olsen reached into an orange bag, suspended by a leather strap around her left forearm, and took out a square piece of parchment. She handed it to Katherine and smiled.

It had the royal seal of the King of Sweden, and her name, "Secretary to the King, Madeline Olsen," was stamped in the middle in raised, gold lettering. Katherine handed it back to the woman.

"Will he provide me with a weapon? I cannot demonstrate unless I have a Winchester rifle." Katherine was already plotting her escape. This was a fortuitous occurrence, but it made sense, as her fame must have spread to Europe by now.

"Most certainly. The king has not come all this way by ship

not to be entertained. Your superintendent, Dr. Rooney, has guaranteed me that you may participate outside. It must be completely private, however. The king has made it quite clear that he wishes to possibly hire you to train his female recruits in the art of sniper warfare."

Katherine was quite overjoyed. At long last, her talents were being respected, in the manner she believed they deserved.

"Just tell me when and where, and I will be there."

"You shall be notified anon. I am very glad to have met you, Mrs. Yantis. I will forward your response to the king. You are assisting women in their quest to gain the militant skills worthy of the Amazons. May God bless you and keep you."

Miss Olsen turned around and began to walk toward the door. The four other female patients stared at her as if she were a specter out of a dream. Miss Lisa Wilkinson pinched herself. Jessica Adkins crept-up behind her and felt her dress from behind. Kitty Reyes sang a song about lost love, and Angela Thoma, awakening from a bad dream, screamed aloud.

When the door was finally shut and locked, Lisa spoke to Katherine. "If you believe all that, then I have a bridge in Brooklyn, New York, I want to sell you."

Jessica

Whenever possible, Jessica preferred to stay near the light. Inside the private room for the five women chosen by Dr. Rooney as special studies for Francis Galton, the fourteen-year-old brunette was huddled beneath the window ledge, staring out at the others. Her blue eyes darted from one face to the next, expecting one of them to remonstrate her for being there, just as they had when she fought them to have the bed closest to the window.

It was her belief that her best friend, Sarah, had commanded her to be on constant guard against all outsiders who would take away her gift of dream. Jessica Adkins dreamed everything around her. She knew once her imagination took over, the details of daily life could change. It was this private change that was the only certainty, Sarah had told her, in one of their frequent philosophical discussions. Sarah's boyfriend, Dennis Leary, never acknowledged Sarah's gift of genius, but Jessica had.

"What you dream is what is real," Sarah had informed her, on that lazy summer day. They sat together upon a large branch of a sugar maple tree in the front garden of Sarah's mansion on Rincon Hill.

Her parents, Richard and Elouise Fremont, had come from England to San Francisco in the 1850s to help finance the Gold Rush. A banker and investor, like Jessica's own father, Raymond, Mr. Fremont helped invest in the newly established bank, Wells Fargo, and hired Raymond as its first manager.

The two families, the Fremonts and the Adkins, lived next-door to each other in the wealthy neighborhood. Jessica and Sarah loved doing things only boys were supposed to do, and tree-climbing was the least dangerous activity they enjoyed.

Sarah had once suspended Jessica by her ankles from the back of a cable car going up California Street to Nob Hill. A much stronger and taller girl, Sarah helped Jason, their Irish butler, cut wood, and she knew how to ride a horse when she was five. The day she told Jessica about dreaming, she was being harassed by Dennis, and the girls had climbed the tree to escape him.

Jessica's daily adventures with Sarah were a ritualized performance. To her, Sarah was both a mentor and a spiritual adviser, so when she informed Jessica that she was dreaming her own, and all of the world's, existence, she believed her at once.

"You mean, everything around me is being imagined by my mind?" Jessica asked her friend on that fateful day.

"Oh, yes! The truth is, each of us believes he or she is dreaming a private reality, and it's true. There is no shared existence whatsoever. There are only accidental meetings and coincidental rendezvous, which each dreamer creates inside her own vivid imagination."

Sarah picked a large leaf from the branch and held it in front of Jessica's wide eyes. "See? I am dreaming this leaf, and every event that happens around it. You see it too but only because our dreams have intersected for a brief time. When we separate, only our separate dream-weaving will exist."

Sarah then told sixteen-year-old Dennis that she no longer wanted to dream him, and he became enraged. He was at the base of the tall tree, staring up into the branches at the two girls.

"I will show you who is imaginary!"

Dennis began to climb the tree, and as he did so, Sarah began to climb as well. Jessica watched, in fascination, as her best friend ascended ever higher in the tall maple, stepping on a branch, pulling herself up, and then reaching for the next, higher branch.

Dennis kept up his chase, however, and soon Jessica could see them both above, suspended precariously, in the highest branches. The next words she heard from Sarah would live forever in her dream world. As her friend reached out, Jessica looked up through the branches into the summer sky on Rincon Hill. Dennis reached out to grab onto Sarah, but she would not accept his touch.

"Our dreams have met, and now they shall be over!" Jessica watched, in abject horror, as Sarah fell from the tree. She landed on the hard ground, her neck breaking her fall, and her limp body tumbled down the hill.

As she climbed down from the tree, branch by branch, Jessica began to believe. Everything around her became more vivid and more important to her. She understood that her destiny, and the destiny of the entire world, were inside her imagination. That summer's insight became Jessica's passionate fixation forever.

Jessica dreamed the man with the lamb-chop sideburns and the pointy upper lip. He had come into the room, escorted by her imaginary doctor named Mister Rooney. They were both standing above her, looking down, and she knew she could make them disappear at once, simply by closing her eyes. She decided to listen to them, just to see what she could invent next.

The older man with the strange accent addressed her. "Hello, Jessica. There is another young lady I want you to meet. Her name is Polly Bedford. She can also dream and talk to spirits. I am certain you'll be great friends."

Jessica saw him wink over at Dr. Rooney. *Why did I make him do that? He sounds very interesting. I'll have to ask Sarah the next time I see her.* "I can make you all disappear, you do realize that? However, because I am becoming very bored with these old women in here, I shall go with you to meet her."

"Jolly good!" The old man reached down, took Jessica's hands, and pulled her up. Jessica dreamed what he then said, and she smiled at him when he said it. "You will both be changing what we all dream. I can assure you of that. We shall come for you once we arrange the meeting with Miss Bedford."

Melissa

Melissa was exhausted. She wondered why she had to waste her precious time conversing with idiots. When she finally broke her vow of silence to speak to the older married woman, Katherine, Pepper immediately decided to go back into her perpetual mummery. These reprobates did not deserve her wisdom. Let them succumb to the patriarchal establishment that was controlling their destinies inside this mad house. She was going to become the avenger of women everywhere, and to this end, she might have to endanger them, not to mention putting her own genius in jeopardy.

"Wilkinson! Come out here at once!"

The voice was obviously summoning her from beyond the room's enclosure. Did they really believe she was stupid enough to go out into that snake pit? And yet, something about the masculine baritone of that voice made her body quiver with sexual interest. It sounded like her departed husband, Jeremy's voice.

If she could change anything from the past, she would have not stabbed her poor husband on their wedding night. He was not to blame for the insane logic of the times. He did not create the lust, the greed, and the constant mayhem of living under a system dominated by the male hierarchy. Jeremy's hands were gentle, his touch sublime, and he was the first person to call her "Pepper." She stabbed him out of an ocean of resentment built inside her soul. He was the dead canary within her coal mine of hate for much greater and more powerful evils.

"Pepper! Won't you come out? I have unlocked the door for

you."

Melissa watched the other four women. Nobody lunged forward to escape. They all just stared at the door like the lunatics they indeed were.

"All right. I'm coming. If you harm me, then you will forever be haunted by my evil spirit." Melissa believed this curse, as she moved toward the door. Before opening it, she stared out through the wire mesh rectangle. Nobody was out there. Could the door be unlocked?

She reached down and turned the knob. It turned a full turn, and she heard the necessary click, releasing the lock. The heavy door opened, squealing its usual resistance. When she discovered no person out in the hallway, she turned around and peered inside from whence she came.

"Come on, ladies! What are you waiting for? It's our chance." Melissa realized she had broken her vow of silence once more, and that was when a shadow came out of the passageway, and she saw a long arm push the door shut, with a grunt coming from the man who had slammed it.

The tall man, dressed in all-black, grabbed her by her right arm and pulled her—dragged her—along the hallway. When he came to a room, she saw that it had a number, "13." He unlocked it with a key he extracted from his waistcoat pocket. She stared at the back of his head. He had black hair, and his cheeks were shaved.

"Quickly, get inside, Pepper. I need to tell you something."

That voice again. She was mesmerized by it. The inside of the room was grimy and dank. It was one of the few unused rooms in the asylum, with stacks of flour, wheat and other cooking supplies and foodstuffs. It smelled of disinfectant and yeast.

Melissa took a good look at this man. He was clean on his face, and his dark brown eyes penetrated her being the way Jeremy's used to do. It was like being breached sexually, but she had never gotten to that. She had left Jeremy frustrated and staring quizzically at the bloody knife she held in her hand that night after their church wedding.

"I want you to have this," the young man said. He extracted

a leather strap with something dangling at the end. He held the large, oval medallion up to her eyes in the dark room. "It belonged to the Empress Dowager of China." She saw the design on the silver backing. It was the shape of a swirling dragon, with tiny jewels inserted as the eyes and over the body of the snake-like demon.

"Here is the answer to its secret identity." He grasped the bottom of the medallion with his right thumb and forefinger and pulled. To her surprise, a six-inch steel blade came into her view.

Why would this man give her this? Was it a trap? She would surely be placed in solitary confinement should she accept this weapon of death.

As he placed the sheathed medallion around her neck, and tucked it under her asylum smock, he did the unspeakable. He nuzzled his smooth chin against her neck, kissing it warmly, and with passion.

"I am a prisoner, just as you are, Pepper. I know all about you. You want to stop the real killers who oversee this mad house. I have been entrusted by Francis Galton and Dr. Rooney to trick you into murdering someone on these premises. You shall not stab anyone until I give you further instructions. I trust you will not. Why? Because your entire family will then die. We must learn that we are working for a higher cause. When I give you the order to kill, we can then escape, and I will take my brothers with us. When the time comes, do not listen to anyone else."

As his strong arms turned her around, he gazed into her eyes, and then she watched his lips, and they came down to hers, sucked the air from her lungs, and then gently moved up to her eyes, kissing them closed, up to her forehead, delicately placing lip pressure upon her third, also hidden, eye. This man understood the power of persuasion, and she loved him for it. Despite his words, she knew she could find a way to trick him, if need be, as it was always a constant struggle against such passionate desires that made her what she was.

"I will explain to you how I came from a life very similar to yours, and we will soon become closer as a result. For now, I shall return you to your prison, and I shall return to mine."

Chapter 7: Lost Souls

The Women's Section, First Floor, Stockton State Insane Asylum, Morning, April 26, 1887.

The first investigations would now begin, and Clara was inside their private room, seated with her notes, at a small desk in the middle of the room beside a Franklin stove. The men, Dr. Andrew McFarland, and her lover, Captain Isaiah Lees, were sharing one bunk bed in an enclosed area next to the bathroom. Mrs. Packard had her own bed, with a wood plank for her back beneath the mattress. Clara and her best friend, Ah Toy, were sleeping in the bunk bed next to the door. Laura de Force Gordon was sharing the final bunk bed with Dr. McFarland's granddaughter, Anne, next to Clara and Ah Toy. In deference to their group's privacy, Laura had already left the room for breakfast.

Clara realized she would need to better coordinate communications now that her group of investigators had dwindled to six. The other member was her friend and rival attorney, Laura Gordon, but she was playing the role of friendly adversary. Clara wanted to use her friend as a devil's advocate for the group's thinking, since Laura represented the interests of the Cotton family. Since both Adeline and Bertha were working undercover, one of the first items on the agenda was to figure a method of communicating with them inside the asylum. Adeline had already informed them that she was working for Francis Galton and not Leland Stanford.

Finally, the news that Superintendent Dr. Alfred Rooney brought to them the day before made Clara wary. He said Governor Bartlett had approved Stockton asylum as an extension for mental health research at Stanford's new university. That meant it would be more difficult to investigate the activities of Galton and his group. If they were indeed connected to the murder of Winnifred Cotton, then it meant the source of the conspiracy could be right there, under their noses. As they were sniffing downstairs, the real culprits could be upstairs planning more insidious activities.

"May I have your attention?" Clara watched her colleagues, as they were in various stages of dressing. The two men were, of course, unseen behind what Clara was calling the "Wall of Jericho," a long blanket suspended on a clothes line in front of the bunks. When she heard an assortment of grunts and responses from them all, she continued. "Today, I would like Dr. McFarland and Anne to interview the physicians concerning the medications administered in the facility. We would like to see if the drugs being prescribed are appropriately matched to the patients who must take them. Ah Toy, you and I shall question the nursing and household staff." Clara cupped her hands around her mouth and shouted, "Mrs. Packard? I want you to interview all the residents on the first floor. Try to assess their relationships and their mental stability, especially as it pertains to the drugs being given."

All of them were now dressed, and they stood around Clara at her table. The women decided to wear the same clothing as the female patients; the simple, navy-blue frock pull-overs. Captain Lees adjusted his Colt 45 in its holster around his hairy chest, beneath a red shirt tucked into blue denims, which was the uniform worn by the male patients of the asylum. These men were housed in another wing. The Bowie knife Isaiah usually carried was not worn in deference to a patient Dr. Rooney described to Clara as a "murderess who stabbed her husband to death."

Dr. McFarland, despite being a grandfather of sixty-four, stood tall and straight, with gray, curly hair and a ruddy, Irishman's complexion. His granddaughter was an intellectual sort, with spectacles, and her brown hair was in a neat bun.

"I want to thank you, Dr. McFarland, and your granddaughter, Anne, for lending your expertise to our cause. If we can discover who was responsible for the murder of Winnifred Cotton, we believe her death may also be related to this institution and how it is run. The drugs being given to Polly Bedford, in fact, may be the connection we need, so your assessment of her is very important to our case." Clara smiled up at them.

"Thank you, Mrs. Foltz. If there are any shenanigans about, you may rest assured we will uncover them." Dr. McFarland took Anne's hand. "As for the methodology of the asylum, my granddaughter is an expert at finding all the accounting and other tricks such organizations have for hiding their misdeeds."

"I am certain you will, as my esteem for Liz Packard is such that her recommendation of you both is quite sufficient." Clara stood up from the desk and took in a deep breath. "Shall we briefly discuss how to make our contacts with our two spies? Bertha and Adeline need safe havens in which to impart their information."

Mrs. Packard, who now had her collapsible hearing aid, nodded her head. "Yes, I believe I saw a place that may suit your needs, detective Foltz. I was escorting Dorothy, the patient I found wandering the halls the other night. She informed me that the angels came down in the morning during breakfast. When I asked her where these cherubs might be, she showed me a trap door in the ceiling beneath the staircase. It pulls down by a lever, and there are stairs leading up into a portion of the attic used for storage. I believe if you should rendezvous with your daughters up there, it would be safe. You could place someone at the bottom to be a look-out."

Clara chose not to explain to Liz that Adeline was not her daughter, as yet, but the idea struck her as quite good. "Yes, that could work very well, Liz. Thank you. We will use that means and call it by the code name Jacob's Ladder."

"I suggest you make certain you're already up there first," Isaiah pointed out. "Your helper could then open the door for your guest, and stand guard while you're both up there conducting business."

"Bravo! I can see why we have you on our committee, Captain. I have read about your detective exploits in the newspapers." Dr. McFarland slapped Isaiah on the back.

"Isaiah has instructed me in the finer arts of sleuthing, and for that I am forever indebted to him." Clara pulled down at the waist of her patient's frock, as she was self-conscious about her weight. Her daughters, especially Bertha, were often reminding of her extra baggage. "Shall we adjourn to breakfast in the dining hall? Afterward, we can begin our appointed rounds. I wish you all the best of luck, and may God be with us."

"Please remember," Anne McFarland said, bringing her hands together at the mention of prayer. "These are lost souls. They can only be rescued by the grace of a higher power. We are merely conduits to lead them back to our Maker's orderly universe, where they may hopefully join us once more in our daily struggles."

"Amen," Ah Toy said, and Clara smiled at her. She then followed her Taoist friend out the door, followed closely behind by the others.

***

The Women's Section, Second Floor, Stockton State Insane Asylum, Afternoon, April 26, 1887.

Bertha May Foltz was spying on the conversation between Francis Galton and Dr. Rooney. The scientist did not trust Adeline, as she was able to read his thoughts, so Bertha was chosen to be the spy. Elizabeth Packard, who was interviewing patients that day on the first floor, had also informed Bertha of the clandestine hiding place wherein she and Adeline were to meet, individually, in order to communicate directly with Mrs. Foltz about what was happening upstairs.

After infiltrating the second floor by a dumbwaiter used to send food from the kitchen to the second-floor rooms, Bertha was now using that dumbwaiter to listen in on Galton and Rooney. She leaned against the plywood door with her ear pressed against it.

"We have set the wheels in motion for all my experiments, Alfred. Phase two will begin tomorrow." Bertha could tell the voice of Mr. Galton, as it had the British pronunciation of words.

"How did you establish your link to each of my patients? Also, what will happen in phase two? Perhaps, one day, I shall write my own book concerning the experiments we have conducted." That

85

was Rooney's voice. She would know that raspy, Irish baritone anywhere.

Bertha could hear papers being shuffled. "Let me see. Here we are. Subject 1, Miss Sidney Reyes. My conjoined twins have established the necessary lustful attraction, and Susanne tells me she should soon have complete control over this Filipina's mind. In phase two, I want to see if that control can lead to murder."

Murder? Bertha's pulse began to race. *If these men want to create murderers, then perhaps they are behind the murder of Polly's friend, Winnie Cotton.*

"You can't mean you will allow her to kill in my asylum. We just gained approval from Governor Bartlett . . ."

"No, you idiot. She will not kill anyone. I just want to see how far her hereditary rebelliousness goes. This will allow us to establish the necessary causal proof we need to show the Congress of the United States why we need to change the laws immediately to protect the safety of society's elite."

"I see. Now I understand. And, what about the second patient? Mrs. Angela Thoma?"

"I had my psychic assistant, Miss Quantrill, impersonate a voice from the dead to arouse this woman's sick psyche into a state of suspended belief. She can now be easily manipulated by this means, and the same test will be applied to her."

"Attempted murder?"

"Correct."

Bertha's heart was now racing. She knew she had to get this information to her mother as soon as possible. She twisted inside the small compartment, and the box she was in dropped slightly on the pully, making a squealing sound. *Good God in Heaven! They will find me!*

"Did you hear that?" It was Francis Galton's voice.

"No. What was it?"

"It sounded as if it was coming from that wall."

"Oh. Correct. The kitchen staff uses that dumbwaiter to send up food to our wealthy patients and to our room. It's close to lunch, and they're probably sending something."

"Jolly good. I am getting rather famished."

Bertha exhaled and held her stomach, which was beginning to gurgle at the mention of lunch. *This blasted dumbwaiter and my own stomach are turning against me!*

"Please. Finish your explanation. Then we can eat something."

"Patient number three, Katherine Yantis. My Swedish solo triplet, Deandra, shall impersonate King Oscar's personal secretary. At the rendezvous, Mrs. Yantis will be tested to determine if she can kill with a Winchester repeating rifle."

"Oh, good. I shall have my staff prepare for this meeting with the king. Who will get to play Oscar?"

"Why, with a bit of physical alteration, I think you would make an excellent royal personage, don't you?" Bertha pictured Dr. Rooney as a king, and she shuddered at the image. He already had complete power over all the men and women in this asylum. As a king, what would he do, pray tell?

"Thank you, Francis. I will forever be indebted to you!"

"The fourth woman, the girl, Jessica Adkins. She has agreed to meet with Polly Bedford. I have a drug I've been testing, and I shall use it on the Adkins girl. With her present psychosis, we can see how far we can extend her dream world. Hopefully, it will enter into homicidal tendencies."

"What is this drug called? I don't believe I am familiar with such a pharmaceutical. It would seem it could be used in our military, for good purpose, no doubt."

"Hardly. This drug has sparked wars on the Asian continent between my own country and China. Combined with an already hysterical mind, like that of young Adkins, opiates prove to be the most conclusive prescription for homicidal ideations."

"How interesting! Why didn't I think of that? I suppose this is because the drug is used in so many legal medicines, such as laudanum. Our Congress will certainly want to know how murders might be increasing because of its use."

"Yes, well, we have a specific purpose in mind, don't we? We need not tell the authorities that our young lady was given such medication before she tried to kill Polly Bedford."

Kill Polly? These men are plotting bold experiments, indeed!

"I am almost afraid to ask about Mrs. Wilkinson. She has already killed. What purpose do you have in mind for her?"

"Ah, yes. My lone identical triplet, Mr. Claiborne Falcone, has enamored the woman with his masculine charms. He has also given her a weapon and a purpose. What she does not know is that the weapon is harmless. The tin it is made from is constructed to fall apart once it is used. We shall, however, have proof that her hereditary disposition can move her to kill once more, very easily."

"How ingenious! This will give us five demonstrated tests to prove our case to Congress."

When Bertha heard the dumbwaiter door being opened, she fumbled for the pulley with which to descend, but she was not fast enough. The face of Francis Galton, his pointed upper lip quivering, was staring at her. "Put this girl in isolation. Immediately!" She felt his arms encircle her body and yank her forward into his arms. Bertha was most saddened because she would not be able to inform her mother; and her sister and brother, Trella and Samuel, would be ashamed to be related to her.

"Who is this girl?" Francis Galton was watching Dr. Rooney, as he grasped Bertha by her arm.

"Deidra Watkins. She was admitted last week. We found her wandering around Golden Gate Park in a transfixed state. She has no parents or relatives that we could locate." The Superintendent grabbed her by the shoulders. "She could be a malefactor. Miss, why were you in there?"

Bertha thought she might be able to talk her way around this capture by using her wit and guile. "I am friends with Polly Bedford, sirs. She told me she saw who the killer of Winnie Cotton was. I knew the nurses wouldn't let me come up here, so I used the dumbwaiter to reach your room."

"Oh, is that so? Quite interesting. And who would this perpetrator be? Be informed. If your evidence proves to be invented, you will never see the light of day again." Dr. Rooney twisted her arm, and Bertha winced in pain.

"She said it was Samuel Foltz, her neighbor on Nob Hill." Bertha kept her face unemotional and grave, just the way she had seen her mother speak before a jury in a San Francisco court room.

Francis Galton's bushy eyebrows rose on his forehead. "Foltz? Is he a relative of our inquisitor downstairs? Attorney Clara Foltz?"

"Yes, he is. He's her son." Dr. Rooney loosened his grip on Bertha's arm, leaving a red mark on the skin. "I read about him in the *Chronicle*. He assisted Clara Foltz in her case concerning the mesmerist murders of wealthy husbands."

"We may be able to end this committee's investigation and also establish a criminal motive of the utmost importance to state authorities." Galton raised his right hand's thumb and forefinger to his chin. "Of course, we shall have to bring this young Foltz in for questioning at once."

"Wait a moment, sir, if you don't mind. Can't we use this important information in another way?" Dr. Rooney touched Galton's forearm.

"Another way? What does your Yankee ingenuity have in mind?"

"We could turn Samuel into a spy for us. If he did kill Miss Cotton, then we can dispose of him later. If he did not, but he is too afraid that we shall tell his mother, then he will certainly work for us."

"I know a better way, Dr. Rooney. My employee, Adeline Quantrill, is in love with this Samuel Foltz. She told me so. Her job with me is her way to impress Mrs. Foltz and her family so that she can become worthy of their respect."

"That's very interesting. Please, go on."

"We can tell Mr. Samuel Foltz that unless he works for us, his love, Adeline, will receive the worst employment review that has ever been created by a scientist of my stature." Galton smiled. "That should make him work for us with no qualms whatsoever. And, as you say, if he proves to be the murderer of Winnifred Cotton, then we can indeed turn him over to the authorities at the conclusion of our experiments."

Bertha's mind was spinning. Was she still going to be put into isolation? Would she be able to tell the others before Samuel began to work for these scoundrels?

"What about our little intruder? Hasn't she heard too much?" Dr. Rooney again took Bertha's forearm in his vice-like grip.

"Yes, she must be placed in solitary confinement until we can execute our plan. Take her away."

***

The Women's Section, First Floor, Stockton State Insane Asylum, Evening, April 26, 1887.

Clara was happy the day was over. She and Ah Toy interviewed the entire staff of seventeen nurses and other employees, but other than hearsay allegations of alleged cruelty toward some patients, there were no leads about activities which could prove to a court of law that the asylum should be closed down. The others in her group were assembled at the doctors' table inside the dining hall. The patients on the first floor had previously been fed, as well as the staff physicians and nurses. Clara's group was privately dining on roast brisket of beef, mashed potatoes, garden carrots, and salad.

"Liz, how did your day progress? Were you able to inform Bertha concerning Jacob's Ladder?" Clara purposely sat next to Mrs. Packard, so as to be within close range of her eardrums.

"Yes, she is now aware, and she told me she informed Adeline Quantrill upstairs. It seems they have surreptitiously arranged another endeavor on their own during lunch. I am not privy as to its details, purpose, or goal, however." Mrs. Packard cut into her meat, in the European tradition, with her knife held in her right hand, and her fork in her left. She brought the meat to her mouth and nodded. "Quite good. Rare, the way I prefer."

"Dr. McFarland and Anne? What about your questions of the doctors on staff? Any skullduggery afoot?" Clara dabbed her cloth napkin to her lips.

"We went over the patient records and matched them with the script from the doctors. Nothing untoward as yet. Anne and I still want to interview the pharmacist. Sometimes, in these cases, there can be a secret arrangement being made that's quite illegal." Dr. McFarland sipped from his wine glass.

"Isaiah, what about your rounds? Have you discovered any inappropriate activities?"

"No. I was accosted by several women, however. I suppose my male uniform harkened them back to the Christmas Dance that I'm told allows the sexes to mingle for a night of frivolity. As you are quite aware, dear Clara, I do not dance with my two left feet." Captain Lees chuckled. "Women, especially these women, can be quite forward."

The entire group began to laugh, and soon they were teary-eyed with frivolous entertainment, at the expense of the burly police captain. Clara extended her hand across the table to grasp Isaiah's hand in her own. She smiled at him, and pursed her lips into a pucker of affection.

Chapter 8: The Visitor

The Women's Section, Jacob's Ladder, Stockton State Insane Asylum, Morning, April 27, 1887.

When Clara learned about the incarceration of her daughter, Bertha May, she was inside Jacob's Ladder talking with Adeline. Clara realized her committee needed to increase its pressure on the authorities of the asylum. Dr. Rooney had mentioned that he was going to keep the female, Deidra Watkins, in solitary confinement, so the committee could not interview her anymore. Unless her group discovered a way to overrule Rooney's authority, Bertha would remain in isolation. One less spy for them to use, and perhaps Dr. Rooney might even attempt to torture her daughter for information.

Downstairs, beneath the ladder leading up into the attic storeroom, Captain Lees was holding vigil as their guardian. The light inside the room was a dim reflection coming from a small window on the far side. Clara could barely discern Adeline's face in the shadows, but it was the importance of her information that she was focused upon.

"What has been the motivation of these two men upstairs? Who are these five women, and what do Dr. Rooney and Francis Galton plan to do with them?" Clara was trying to remain calm, as the news about Bertha had increased her tension and fear.

"I am so sorry, Mrs. Foltz. I am not allowed to see these women. Mr. Galton contracted with Dr. Rooney to have them locked in a private room. All I do know is there are going to be experiments done on them."

Clara could tell by the tremors in her young voice that Adeline was quite emotional. "Don't be frightened. However, I am afraid you are now our only link to their endeavors. Until we can come up with some hard evidence to force our way into their research, we will have to rely on what you tell us."

"Only link? What about Bertha May?" Adeline reached out to grasp Clara by her right forearm. "Has she been harmed?"

"Oh, no. Dr. Rooney informed us she was placed in isolation due to some serious infraction of the asylum's rules. Therefore, we have nobody to watch over Polly at the moment. Mrs. Packard is attempting to interview the girl, but there is always a nurse standing by, so her questions are limited." Clara moved next to Adeline and put her arm around her shoulders. "Please continue, dear. We must know whatever you have been able to perceive, including your psychic abilities."

Instead of becoming calmer, Clara could feel Adeline's body begin to shake with emotion. "Francis Galton is also a telepath. He informed me that my psychic talent was one of the major reasons he hired me for this job. He knew I had access to past history. I discovered we could read each other's thoughts when I was being interviewed at Leland Stanford's mansion. I have to be so careful around him, Mrs. Foltz. It is giving me nightmares about being found out. What if they do discover what I am doing? Would they kill me?"

Clara was sorry for the girl's fear, but she knew unless she was completely honest with her, the entire investigation could be placed in jeopardy. "No, not unless they are directly responsible for the murder of Winnie Cotton. We have no reason to believe they are, at this point. Although, we do have suspicions that their overall philosophy toward the mentally ill may be suspect. What can you tell me about that?"

"They don't allow me to be there during their conversations. I am presently a tutor and ward of the identical triplets."

"Identical triplets? Who are they?" Clara was quite surprised by this new revelation.

"Two sets of identical triplets. They came from Europe and

93

Scandinavia with Mr. Galton. Two in each set are conjoined from birth defects. One each is not, but they were all born identical in appearance and mere minutes apart. The three males are named Falcone, and they're from Scotland. And the three females are named Johansen, and they come from Sweden. They are quite nice, actually, and we get along with each other very well."

"How is Galton using them? Are they being questioned, or are there formal scientific experiments? Are they being harmed in any manner?" Clara thought this might be a key to being able to intervene upstairs with their investigating committee.

"I don't know. Mr. Galton calls for each separately, except for the conjoined set, and then they all reappear later in the day inside our room. They tell me nothing about what they're doing, except for one. His name is Claiborne. When I first met him, he told me he and his brothers were Jews, with the given surname of Feldman. Claiborne says he believes Mr. Galton to be a madman and that Mr. Feldman is staying in the asylum only to protect the others."

Clara was intrigued. "What proof does he have that Francis Galton is insane?"

"He has stopped talking about that. Claiborne has gone back into a shell of conformity for some reason. I shall keep trying to get him to tell me. Do you think I should tell him what I am really doing working for Galton?"

"No. Don't do that. We can't know at this point whether or not this young man is simply trying to bring you out at the behest of Galton's private instructions. Just keep watching him." Clara stepped back. "Anything else? I need to return to my group downstairs."

"There's to be a visitor today. Dr. Rooney informed us. A psychiatrist from Munich, Germany, by the name of Dr. Emil Kraepelin. They will be giving him a tour of the asylum and discussing European standards of care."

Clara believed this might be a break in their investigation they had waited for. "I must discuss this with my group, especially with Dr. McFarland and Elizabeth Packard. In the meantime, try to spy on them to overhear what they say. I know, I am putting you at risk, but this may be very important to our case. Can you do that for me?" Clara again grasped Adeline's arm.

"Yes, I can do that. You have done more than that for me. I will report back to you after he is given the grand tour. Please tell Samuel that I miss him."

"I shall, my dear, and thank you for being our spy in the sky. We can rendezvous here at the same time, after breakfast, tomorrow."

"Goodbye," Adeline said, and Clara began to walk back toward the ladder. "Mrs. Foltz?"

"Yes?" Clara turned around.

"I dreamed about you last night. You were visiting me, here, in our private room. You were conjoined with Samuel. Francis Galton was standing behind you both, and he told us you were his most recent experiment."

Clara laughed. "That is indeed a bold experiment! My son Samuel would sooner be hitched to a mother grizzly bear, I am afraid." Clara bent down and rapped three times with her knuckles on the trap door. After a few moments, she could hear Isaiah climbing up the steps.

* * *

The Women's Section, Second Floor, Stockton State Insane Asylum, Evening, April 27, 1887.

Bertha May could hear the voices coming down the hall toward her room. For hours, it had remained eerily silent. She never heard anybody, not even the wealthy lunatics who prowled the halls at all hours babbling their incantations. Her fear was not for herself. She was more afraid that Polly Bedford would be harmed in some way. If that happened, then her mother would be furious at her.

She needed to collect herself before these people come into her room. Bertha mussed her hair and decided she would play the game she played with Polly: Mental Metamorphosis. She covered her face with her hands and concentrated. *My insanity can be the*

95

way to invoke the real truth from these visitors. I must think the way mother does. Trickery is in my genetics. When she completed her metamorphosis, and sat up straight on her bed, Bertha had become her sleuthing character, Deidra Watkins, the orphan found wandering alone in Golden Gate Park.

The door opened with a squealing groan. Three men entered, and Bertha already knew two of them, but the third man, a short, handsome man, with an all-white suit, white hair, gray goatee, and black eyebrows, walked right up to where she was sitting on the edge of the bed. He stared down at her, and she stared up at him, for about three minutes. She was not going to turn away, or be intimidated, no matter what his importance.

"Do you think about why you are here?"

"No. Do you?" Bertha saw, too late, from the corner of her eye, the flat hand, striking at her from the side. She was hit hard, and her head snapped to the right. The skin of her left cheek stung like needles had stuck her, and she knew it would fill with blood, turn a flushed crimson, and leave a ghastly purple bruise.

Dr. Alfred Rooney, who had struck her, was smiling, rubbing his right palm against the front of his frock coat. "We get these types quite often, I am afraid. Our effort to rehabilitate often meets a dead end when it comes to these girls in their teenage years. They wander on their own, so they become hardened by the streets whereupon we find them."

"I understand. However, I find in the clinical setting, the wild ones provide the best testing results." Bertha twisted her head away, when this strange doctor attempted to stroke her cheek with his outstretched hand.

"That is what I am attempting. The five I told you about have been prepared for hereditary experiments." Francis Galton walked over to stand next to the visiting clinician from Germany. "However, this one has told us she overheard one of our patients identifying who the murderer might be in a case involving a young girl from a wealthy San Francisco family. The murdered Cotton girl was one of the transmissible elite we have vowed to protect."

"We have a plan to get this murder suspect, Samuel Foltz,

into the asylum where we can employ him. His mother, Clara Foltz, is the head of the investigating committee about which we told you." Dr. Rooney took out two pairs of steel chain shackles from the inside of his waistcoat. "I am taking you down to see Polly, Miss Watkins. Our first experiment is about to commence. We want you to elicit from her the name of Samuel Foltz as the killer of Winnifred Cotton. Since you were caught spying, we must keep you restrained."

Francis Galton furrowed his brow and turned to address the German. "Do you suggest we allow this girl speak to Polly before we admit our subject, Jessica Adkins, into the room?"

Bertha watched, as Dr. Rooney first put the chains around her wrists, and then, stooping down, encircled her ankles with the second pair.

"One moment. If this Foltz is the murderer of the elite Cotton youth, then why not place him in the room with them both? I find that psychosis can often be broken when the patient experiences the traumatic effect again. Don't you agree?"

"I see what you mean. If Polly Bedford becomes lucid after seeing Samuel Foltz, the killer, again, then she can testify against him in court. Rooney, take those off, and then go pay a visit to young Foltz." Galton walked over to the door. "Emil, please come. We can do the second experiment. She's an actual murderer who stabbed her poor husband on his wedding night. I have followed your advice this time, in that my subject will be given instructions to use a harmless placebo knife on another patient."

"You must keep a full record of what transpires. Our international group will require such proof to move forward."

Bertha watched the three men as they left the room. She knew she had to find a way to escape before Samuel entered the fray. Unless her mother could take action, then she might be representing her own son in criminal court. Why had she put him into this predicament? Did she harbor some kind of sick resentment of her own against Samuel for being their mother's favorite? Perhaps all this time inside the asylum was working to unhinge her mind. Was that it? Bertha walked over to the door and peered through the rectangle of wire mesh. One thing was certain. There was a bigger conspiracy happening than just one murder. This international group must have ideas of its own about why people murder and perhaps become insane enough to attempt murder.

Panic had finally set in. Bertha's plan, before she was caught, was hatched with Adeline Quantrill, inside Jacob's Ladder. They were to go together to spy on Claiborne Falcone, one of the identical triplets being used by Galton in his work. Adeline believed Falcone, whose name actually might be Feldman, could possibly work with them. They needed to get information concerning Dr. Rooney and Francis Galton and what they had planned for these five experiments. Adeline would now have to go it alone until Bertha found a way to escape. Before she could get out of this room, Samuel might have already proved Bertha to be a liar. And then, she thought, they could really have her committed.

***

The Women's Section, Second Floor, Stockton State Insane Asylum, Evening, April 27, 1887.

Melissa Sue Wilkinson was ready. She kept fingering the Chinese medallion around her neck beneath her smock as she sat on her lower bunk near the door. Even though she regretted stabbing her husband, Jeremy, to death, she still had the urge to stab things. The handsome young man who kissed her said she would be able to use the knife soon. She simply had to wait for his instructions. Waiting, however, was not one of Melissa's better character traits.

For example, the other four women in her company were getting on her nerves. They were really much more mentally affected than Melissa could ever become in her wildest dreams. Kitty Reyes, her bunk mate, kept moaning and crooning Philippine love songs in some gibberish language that sounded more like a duck quacking than musical lyrics of lost love. Katherine Yantis was constantly turning on Melissa and pretending to draw guns from an invisible holster around her waist. Kathy even took an apple from lunch and placed it on Kitty's head. One crazy girl singing, and the other one playing Annie Oakley with a rifle. What lunacy!

Oh, and then there were the other two. Melissa almost pulled the blade out of her medallion when Angela Thoma woke her out of a sound sleep one night to tell Melissa there was an evil spirit hovering just above her. Angie then said she was talking to it, and that she could convince the spirit not to kill her, if Melissa would give Angela her portion of potatoes at dinner time. Jessica Adkins was the final straw. She kept telling them all that they were figments of her dream world. The teenager even asked Melissa, while they were bathing, if she would prefer to have larger breasts. If so, Jessica could promptly dream them up for her!

These were the lunatics she had to live with each day, and the experience was enough to send Melissa over the edge. If it was not for the handsome, dark-haired stranger, life would no longer be worth the struggle.

Melissa got up from her lower bunk and walked slowly over to the door. Her thoughts became a muddled mess. She remembered how her Uncle Joseph used to sing to her alone, inside the family's library. Then he began to molest her sexually, and she remembered his hands, everywhere on her twelve-year-old body, and when his actions became bolder, she picked up a letter opener from the library desk, and she stabbed him in the hand.

Inside, something became infused in her psyche that became a way to cope against what she saw as the ever-increasing, daily harassment by the overlords, the dominating males in charge of most everything around her. Her uncle, in his fear of being discovered, never said anything, but Melissa knew there were others, outside the family's domain, that would not stop. They would kill her if she tried to protect herself, so she was ever-vigilant, ever protective of her body, and, most importantly of her mind.

As she gazed out of the rectangular meshed window to the outside hallway, Melissa felt regret that her mind had become so fearful on her wedding night. Jeremy, sweet Jeremy, became just another male intruder. The boiling rage that had built-up over the years had made her snap, she believed, and now she was inside this monstrous place with nowhere to turn, and nobody to talk to who understood.

When those dark eyes appeared at the window, Melissa was thinking about him. *Is it time to act? Are they going to finally accomplish the feat which will ensure their escape from this madhouse forever?*

The lock on the door clicked, and the door swung toward her. Melissa stepped backward, and the dark stranger walked in. He looked around the room at the other women, who stared back at him, as if he were an archangel come to rescue them all from perdition.

His whisper was hoarse, as if he had rehearsed what he was telling her many times. "We must go now. You must do as I say, and you must never hesitate for one second. Our lives depend upon it. My brothers will meet us when we take him hostage."

"Who is him?" Melissa stepped out into the dark hallway, and he shut the door and locked it.

"You shall see. Now. Follow closely behind me."

As she walked behind him, she felt like his shadow. In fact, in her mind, she was sucking in his power, his male animus, and her body become infused with a new energy she had only experienced once before: when she stuck the letter opener in her uncle's hand.

As they came to the corner of a passageway leading into the wealthy patients' dining room, Melissa could see Dr. Rooney standing in the doorway with two other men. They also looked like officials or doctors, and they nodded to her escort.

Dr. Rooney smiled. "Take her inside. Rosemary is waiting. She is one of the elite patients about whom I told you."

Melissa watched him nod at Dr. Rooney, but then, as they walked slowly into the large dining room, he turned around to whisper in her ear. "Slowly, very slowly, pull out the blade. Once you have it in your grasp, you will begin to walk toward the woman inside. Keep the knife out of sight. The men will follow. Move so you are in front of Dr. Rooney and facing her. At the last moment, I want you to turn around and grab the superintendent and hold the knife at his throat. We will use him to get out of here. Do you understand? This is our only chance at freedom!"

The word "freedom" rang inside her being like the cracked bell she once saw in Philadelphia. She had always pictured that bell as an icon for women's rights because it, like most women in the United States, was a used and damaged instrument, ringing out its message of liberty every day, but that message was falling upon mostly deaf ears.

The three men followed Melissa and her escort into the room. About five yards away stood her intended victim. A statuesque damsel with auburn hair, a blue bell bonnet with a matching dress, and tiny, red satin slippers. She was smiling at Melissa as the space between them grew smaller. Melissa held the blade in her hand and glanced back to see where Dr. Rooney was standing. He was about five feet from where Melissa now stood.

"I have the hand of God in my grasp, my dear lady. Do you want to touch the hand of God? Come to me. I will allow you to experience a joy that no human, other than myself, has ever experienced!"

Melissa decided to act before being told. "I can't go through with this! I am ill, and you won't help me?" She turned around, and she held the knife blade limply against her side as she shuffled across to stand in front of the other gentleman wearing a white suit. She had strategically placed herself so that Dr. Rooney's back was facing her back.

"Oh, kind sir, won't you help me?" she cried to the white-haired stranger. Before Dr. Rooney could turn around to see what this strange gentleman was going to tell her, she spun, lifting her knife up so that it was held in her right hand, the sharp side of the blade toward her.

"Achtung!" The man in white yelled, as Melissa grabbed Dr. Rooney around his slim waist and thrust her blade around his neck until it was being held about a half-inch from his jugular vein on the right side.

"Dr. Rooney. You will come with us. We want you to open the main entrance and allow us to leave. If you do this, you will not be harmed." Her dark escort pointed toward the exit from the dining room.

Expecting to push the doctor toward the exit, Melissa tightened her grip on the handle of the blade and spread her legs apart to gain traction in case the other men attempted to lunge at her.

For a few moments, everything went as planned. Melissa shuffled along with Dr. Rooney toward the door and then out into the hallway.

"Stay back!" Her escort ordered the other two men. They did as they were told and stayed behind, as Melissa waltzed with Dr. Rooney and her dark stranger toward the front entrance of the asylum.

From the side, Melissa could see that Dr. Rooney was smiling. Why would he do that? Did he know something they did not know?

"What is going on here?" An old woman walked toward them out of the shadows.

Dr. Rooney regarded her. "Don't worry, Mrs. Packard. This is merely an experiment. The knife is not real."

The knife is not real? How can that be? This was their only chance to escape, and her dark stranger had lied to her? Her mind was again flooded with the insane fury of that night inside the bridal suite, with her newly wed husband, Jeremy. He had also lied to her about being kind and thoughtful. He was forcing her to eat in a "civil manner." She could hear the constant chomping of his own food, and yet he wanted her to eat in a manner he dictated as most proper for a lady. Why was dipping one's food so barbaric? The Swiss had their fondue. The Egyptians ate with their hands. The Chinese had sticks. Proper should be flexible to the person in charge of his or her own mouth; her own body was her own temple, was it not?

"Believe me, Dr. Rooney, that knife *is* real." Her dark benefactor walked over to stand next to her. "Open that door at once!"

Melissa ran her thumb against the sharp edge of the shiny steel blade. It felt real.

"It cannot be real. I gave you the tin blade myself," Dr. Rooney began, and when Melissa felt his body begin to turn around to face her, she took action.

Her left hand grabbed onto the lower face of the superintendent, and she pulled his face to the left, so the right side of his neck was exposed and under tension. With her blade facing forward, she stabbed the neck slightly behind his right ear, jamming the knife in to the hilt. Then, while pulling the knife out, she knew she needed to push forward so she could rip through the arteries and open a hole in the doctor's neck. The blade sliced deeply into the carotid-jugular beneath the skin, and the blood spewed forth, like a visual animation of the red on the flag standing next to the front entrance door.

As Melissa watched Dr. Rooney's body collapse, she saw that her right forearm and shoulder blade were covered in fresh blood. Her eyes were wide as she watched Mrs. Packard walk toward her, smiling, reaching out to her.

"Let me have it, my dear. You must let me have it *now*." The old woman's voice was calm and reassuring. Was she the one who would finally listen? With a questioning, wide-eyed expression, Melissa handed the bloody knife with the dragon handle, once a possession of the Empress Dowager of China, over to the kindly old woman.

The other two men had grabbed onto her dark stranger, and the last thing she heard, as she followed Mrs. Packard out of the main room and into the side room where the other committee members were, was her escort's strained voice.

"I never put that blade in there! This was only an experiment. I am a Jew. They wanted to blame me for this. I know it. They needed another martyr for their insane cause!"

Chapter 9: Right from Wrong

*San Francisco City Hall Courthouse, San Francisco,
Afternoon, April 29, 1887.*

Captain Isaiah Lees immediately took the patient, Melissa Sue Wilkinson, into custody on April 27. She was transported to the jail in Stockton that same day, and this was where it was discovered that she had never stood trial for the murder of her husband, Jeremy. The Wilkinson family was very wealthy, but their money came from gold, so their status in the community was not from heredity, but their influence was certainly applicable when money was the method of reason in the courts. Although she was not judged legally insane, the courts had accepted the payment of ten thousand dollars to transport Melissa to Stockton State Insane Asylum. This was the pleading agreement issued by the judge and arranged by the family's attorney with the Judge for the State of California in San Francisco.

The San Francisco judge, William H. Cathcart, under direct orders from Governor Bartlett, had ordered a special hearing at the courthouse. This hearing was to determine the sanity of the defendant, Melissa Sue Wilkinson. If proved sane at the time of the homicide, she could then be put on trial for First Degree Murder. However, if she were proved insane, she would again be confined to Stockton State Insane Asylum. This time, however, she would be given the official designation of legal insanity, which would place a permanent mark of shame upon her family.

Clara decided to represent Mrs. Wilkinson in the hearing, and this news spread like wildfire in the press. The irony of the case was that the family, because of the shame that an official insanity decree would inflict upon them, did not want Clara to win. They would, in fact, prefer that their daughter be adjudicated sane, and face a murder trial and possible death sentence. Clara thought this was ludicrous, although she understood the reasoning. Social stature was important in San Francisco, and the Wilkinson family was not from a distinguished line of wealth. They had been one of the many families made rich during the brief Gold Rush, in the 1850s; so their social standing, if Melissa were judged insane, would be such that they would not be accepted into the elite echelon of San Francisco clubs, civic groups, and schools.

The State of California believed it had made the best appointment to argue at this special hearing. Laura de Force Gordon had successfully won against her rival, Clara Foltz, in a previous murder trial, even though it was a victory made after an appeal. Gordon was also quite familiar with the insanity plea, as well as with the evidence and characters involved at the scene of the homicide. Therefore, the San Francisco District Attorney's Office had appointed Mrs. Gordon as the lead attorney and state's prosecutor at this hearing.

Clara was inside a locked counsel room, adjacent to the court, with her team of advisors. Captain Isaiah Lees, who had been the arresting officer, was also sympathetic to Clara and Mrs. Packard's cause, so he was there. Mrs. Elizabeth Ware Packard, of course, was an important advisor to Clara, as was her best friend, Ah Toy. As a resident superintendent and psychiatrist in Illinois, Dr. Andrew McFarland was also being used as an expert witness.

Meanwhile, back at the asylum, Adeline Quantrill was now serving as their only undercover spy. Bertha, as well, was still participating, but she was confined, away from the asylum population. And, in a wicked twist of fate, Clara's son, Samuel Cortland, was working at the asylum for Francis Galton. Clara had no idea as yet why he was doing this, but Ah Toy and Trella told her he was probably trying to be close to Adeline, to protect her.

Clara stood at the head of the conference table, with all the paperwork they had assembled in the two days they had prior to the court-mandated insanity hearing spread before her on the table. The research and interviews they accomplished in forty-eight hours had been phenomenal. Clara, Liz Packard, and Dr. McFarland had interviewed their client, Melissa Wilkinson, extensively. They agreed that putting her in front of the judge, to testify, would not be proper, so Clara was going to explain the case for insanity to the court, and she would also call upon Mrs. Packard and Dr. McFarland as expert witnesses.

The main issue Clara wanted to discuss with her group was what they believed Laura Gordon had up her sleeves. Since this was a hearing, and not a trial, they had no access to evidence, other than the witness testimonies that would be given concerning the homicide of Dr. Rooney. These were in the form of sworn affidavits, which Laura and the D. A.'s office had obtained. The judge would have these, and Clara's team had received copies. There was, of course, no public gallery allowed during this hearing, just members of the press, and the court's goal would be to determine if Mrs. Wilkinson was to be tried as a sane woman for the murder of Superintendent Dr. Alfred Rooney. It was Clara's job, of course, to argue that her client was insane when she committed the stabbing. Clara wanted to explain what she was going to be doing so that her expert witnesses understood her overall legal philosophy.

"Thank you for being here, ladies and gentlemen. I know, I have put on my courtly demeanor, but this is the way I argue. Perhaps I maintain my formal elocution because I have no law degree. I will also be using my feminine character and wardrobe, which will, no doubt, irritate Laura Gordon and all the other suffragists who read about this hearing in the newspapers."

Clara tucked the loose end of her white-frilled blouse's collar into the top of her red dress, which had lion-headed gold buttons running down the front. She also wore a full bustle, and a scarlet, ostrich-feathered hat was on the table in front of her. Finally, she would be wearing long black boots when she entered the courtroom. Isaiah had suggested she also carry a riding whip, and should crack it against the floor, as she strode down the aisle. She did not laugh at his attempted humor.

"The court, as we know, will be using the usual study

questions pertaining to an insanity plea. Not only must we prove that our client passes the M'Nagthen Rules test, established in Common Law, but we must also be certain our experts, that's Liz Packard and Dr. McFarland, understand the current prejudices of the courts pertaining to their expertise." Clara picked up a sheet of paper from a folder in front of her. "Have you both read the list I gave you?"

Dr. McFarland nodded. "Yes, in my previous testimonies around the country, I have often spoken to the points made in your list. Having it to study, however, has been quite a boon, and I thank you, Counselor."

Clara was a bit irked that the psychiatrist was attempting to mimic her formal tone. "And you, Liz? Do you understand these points?" Clara saw that Mrs. Packard was using her collapsible hearing trumpet at long last.

"Of course, Clara. When one has had to fight the legal system in order to escape the insane clutches of the asylum, one tends to remember why one was placed there in the first place."

The others chuckled.

Clara cleared her throat and continued. "I intend to remark upon those items which are brought up by our prosecutors, including their expert witnesses, Francis Galton and his visiting doctor from Germany, Emil Kraepelin. This will, of course, be in the form of rebuttals. However, my main argument shall hinge upon proving that our broader society has become such a pernicious and unjust breeding ground for insanity commitments that our client was simply a tiny mote in the public eye, especially when she is compared to the gigantic beam of unfairness blinding the populace from the greed and graft going on, in the background, in the name of mental health care."

Dr. McFarland struck his fist upon the table top. "Hear, hear! I applaud your analogy and your biblical reference, counselor."

"What about number three on your sheet, Clara?" Ah Toy held up the sheet and pointed. "Let me read it. *Careful attention should be paid to ascertaining the nature of the stressors that may have produced the insanity, including any history of an aversion to assume a duty or job to which the individual now must subscribe, especially that of a soldier.* Since Mrs. Wilkinson was never judged insane in her first encounter with the law, and she had no employment, would the prosecution use her quite obviously stressful experience with her husband as a way to prove she was feigning her insanity?"

"Excellent point. I am certain the prosecution, and the judge, for that matter, will not allow that previous altercation to be raised at all. If I attempt to raise it, I know they will object. And, to be truthful, even though we know it's related to Melissa's mental state, it is not relevant to the case at hand and to what we are obligated to show in the M'Nagthen tests." Clara pointed to the list. "Most of these items, as we now know, point to proving that the accused is feigning insanity. We have all gone over these points with Melissa, and she is aware of the methods of the prosecution to prove she is trying to defraud them. Now that she has been examined by the court, we shall see how well our tutoring worked on her."

Clara noticed that Isaiah was squirming in his chair. "Yes, Captain? I see you're uncomfortable."

"This is what irritates me about the court side of justice. It all seems to become an orchestrated Shakespearean drama. We coach our client, they coach their witnesses, and the judge places them inside the ring as if it were a bloody dogfight. Whatever happened to spontaneous truth in the heat of passion?"

Clara frowned down at him. "Must I again explain to you the dynamics of a hearing of this nature? There will be spontaneous truth that will come to light. No matter how much both sides prepare, the moment two adversaries begin to argue, the immediacy of that argument, when the snarls and scratches begin, truth becomes a product of that confrontation. It is the Hegelian dialectic. I admit, in some foreign jurisdictions, as in Europe and Great Britain, the adversarial approach is seen as rather barbaric and crude. Especially our jury trial and our First Amendment interventions. However, since I work within this legal system, I find it most scintillating and appropriate for the times in which we live."

"Well stated, Clara. What do you plan to use to prove the M'Nagthen tests?" Dr. McFarland raised his caterpillar-gray eyebrows, as she knew he was asking because of his own part in this procedure.

"The law states we must prove that, at the time of the committing of the act, Mrs. Wilkinson was laboring under such a defect of reason, from disease of the mind, as not to know the nature and quality of the act she was doing; or, if she did know it, that she did not know she was doing what was wrong. In point of fact, the person who was actually acquitted of murder, Daniel M'Nagthen, in 1843 England, would have been proved guilty under these tests had he been tried under them."

"Do tell. I never knew that." Elizabeth Packard remarked.

Clara's voice was calm and assured. "Yes. I plan to use the argument that our client was not only diseased of the mind so that she knew not what act she was committing, but that she was also so much under the patriarchal pressure of Superintendent Rooney and Francis Galton, that she snapped, in an insane and homicidal rage."

"I understand now. I like the questions you have for me and Mrs. Packard. You have encapsulated the points in this legal test nicely, and our testimonies will now help you prove them."

"I believe we can now adjourn to the courtroom, ladies and gentlemen. Captain Foltz, you may sit in the back, as you are not officially a part of my legal team. Please remember this. I am going to attempt to hitch our legal star onto the dramatic philosophical argument I will extend to the court. Our purpose is to show the court and the world what is happening during California's current mental health crisis—and it is a crisis—and when we are finished, even the powers in Washington shall know what they are really trying to do inside the Stockton State Insane Asylum."

Clara's group applauded, and they all adjourned.

***

Clara Foltz, Esq. strutted down the center aisle of the courtroom, but she was thinking about how she had lost her last two criminal trials due to the prejudice and misogyny that existed in the legal arena. Both she and Laura Gordon understood those problems to be faced by women who wanted to argue cases before an all-male jury, a male judge, and a mostly patriarchal press and audience. Still, they persisted in their jobs because they believed that one day, when society awakened from its mummification created by hundreds of years of keeping women away from powerful appointments in the public and private sectors, the sexes would be seen as equal, under the law.

At the front of the room, on the right, her friend Laura was seated with her witnesses, two of whom she knew, and one of whom she did not. Laura was wearing her usual plebeian court attire, navy blue dress with no ornaments, no hat, no gloves, no fashionable female accoutrements. Laura saw herself as a woman of the people, and even her arguments were made with that kind of firm, masculine resolve and spirited delivery. Clara, on the other hand, kept her tone intellectual and even feminine, in a polite manner, even though she always used her tall attractiveness and fashionable attire as a way to lull her opposition into a state of calm reflection. Clara believed humans were more prone to agree when their passions were not riled up, and Laura believed the opposite.

"Good morning, Mrs. Gordon. Mr. Galton. Dr. Kraepelin." After they acknowledged Clara with a nod, she turned back to her side of the courtroom where Ah Toy, Dr. McFarland, and Elizabeth Packard sat awaiting her. She took off her hat and placed it gently on the table, and then she looked up at the bench at Judge Cathcart, who was perusing documents, his pince-nez reading glasses suspended at the tip of his nose like mirrors leading into Alice's Wonderland. She knew nothing of his politics or his reputation for being strict or liberal. She did not bother with this type of research. In her experience, the court could be quite prejudiced, and no amount of logic was going to change the verdict. Such had been her recent trial experience representing the Chinese journalist, George Kwong. This had been a kangaroo court wherein she had lost her battle even before she presented her case. Since this was just an insanity hearing, Clara believed she stood a better chance at winning.

"Attorneys for the state and defense, please approach the

bench." Judge Cathcart announced.

Both Clara and Laura got up from their seats and walked down the center of the aisle to look up at the judge. There were only the two sides inside the courtroom. It was empty of visitors, except for the press, who had assembled in the upstairs gallery and were hanging over the railings, notepads and cameras in hand, staring down at the activities like the hungry vultures that they were. They must have looked so ravenous that the judge recognized this.

"Ladies and gentlemen of the press! I must warn you before we begin. No camera photos until I give you permission, and no ruckus or noises, no matter how emotional you may feel about what is being argued. If I have reason to believe you have reported any untruths about these proceedings, I shall ban you from future coverage in the San Francisco City Hall."

The press mumbled acquiescence in low tones, and then were silent, staring down at them with eager attention.

"Assistant District Attorney Gordon, have you assembled all of your witnesses, and are you prepared to present in this matter of the defendant, Mrs. Melissa Sue Wilkinson?"

"I am, your honor." Laura nodded, and then she turned around to stare directly at the one witness Clara did not know.

"Your honor, may I enquire as to the identity of the third witness, sitting next to our German visitor? Mrs. Gordon failed to inform me of him." Clara wanted this information right away, and she was rather aggravated she had not been informed earlier.

"His name is Claiborne Falcone, your honor. I did not include his name because he was not a factor in this presentation until this morning. He has volunteered to provide eye-witness testimony that figures rather importantly on this insanity hearing." Laura smiled at Clara, and it was the smile of the Cheshire cat variety she knew so well. It meant her friend was attempting to sneak something past her.

"I object, your honor. We have not had time to resolve his identity or to ask questions of him. Can this be fair to my client?" Clara kept her tone diffident and warm.

"I understand, Mrs. Foltz. The court will allow you to ask

questions of this witness, and Mrs. Gordon shall provide you with his written testimony, which has just now been given. From what I can tell, he was at the scene of the homicide, and, in fact, he played a significant part in the entire experiment." Judge Cathcart stared down at his paper. "I shall allow his personal testimony based on reflection, as it is crucial to the state's argument."

"Thank you, judge. We are now ready to present our case." Laura turned around and swaggered confidently to the podium in front of the court.

Clara took the paper from Laura and almost ran back to her comrades. She knew that only Mrs. Packard, from her team, had been present during the homicide, and only she would know who this man was and what he was doing on the day in question. Clara handed the paper to Elizabeth, let her read it, and then listened.

"Yes, he was there. From what I know, he is one of Francis Galton's patients. He is from Scotland, and he is one of three identical triplets. Two of them are conjoined, and they are serving to help Galton and the late Dr. Rooney in their experiments." Mrs. Packard sighed. "Doctors attempting to make names for themselves in the field of mental health. I suggest you question them sternly about their purposes, Clara."

Clara was worried about this turn of events. "I shall, but I know my friend. She does not present last minute witnesses unless she believes she has her opponent over a barrel of some sort."

"Your honor, my two expert psychiatrists have examined the defendant, and their conclusions are based on established president concerning whether or not an individual passes the M'Nagthen tests. I am here to argue that not only is the insanity defense a miscarriage of justice, it is also a tactic that was originally established by a court in England. My main witness, Francis Galton, is well aware of how the courts in England work. As his testimony will show, the recent scientific advancements that occurred after the publication of Charles Darwin's research have now been adapted by the mental health community. We shall demonstrate that the defendant, Mrs. Melissa Wilkinson, was quite sane on the day in question. In fact, she was so deliberate in her actions that the other legally insane women in her room were frightened of her. Deliberation of intent, as we in the legal profession understand, is the prime requisite in any criminal case involving the *mens rea* factor. The defendant knew exactly what she was doing when she methodically and viciously stabbed the knife into Dr. Andrew Rooney's throat. It was no fantasy. It was no figment of her crazed imagination in some alternative reality. It was a cold and calculated action based on her hatred and her conviction that the so-called patriarchal powers of society were out to keep her from living her rather obviously antisocial lifestyle. May I please call my first witness, Mr. Francis Galton?"

"Francis Galton, please approach the bench to be sworn in."

The middle-aged appointee of Leland Stanford got up slowly from the State's table and walked over to the bailiff, who was standing near the witness stand, next to the flags of California and the United States.

"Please place your right hand on this Bible." The portly bailiff, in civilian clothes, extended the Bible to him. "Do you, Francis Galton, citizen of the United Kingdom, vow to tell the truth, the whole truth, and nothing but the truth, so help you God?"

"I do."

"Please be seated." The bailiff pointed to the riser where the padded chair was, and Galton climbed the two steps and sat down.

Laura walked over to him and smiled. "Thank you for being here, Mr. Galton. I know you are very active in your work with patients at the Stockton Asylum, and it this work that I want to ask you about."

"Your honor? What does this witness's activity as a researcher have to do with the insanity of my client?" Clara was a bit surprised that Laura would go in this direction. She suspected only a discussion of the events on the day of the alleged murder.

Laura turned and addressed Judge Cathcart. "Your honor, this witness is one of the most renowned scientists in the world. In point of fact, his research was quoted by Charles Darwin in his second text, and he has traveled to do his research almost as extensively as his cousin. Mr. Galton's testimony about his experiments will help prove the sanity of the defendant. Indeed, it will also help to instruct the United States on how to address the increasing epidemic of mental diseases, which now are plaguing this great nation of ours."

"Objection overruled. You may proceed, Mrs. Gordon."

Clara took out her papers concerning Francis Galton and his qualifications. She was ready to rebut his testimony, but she knew she would need to extend her points to meet the wider range of discussion. The points she could not address she would refer to Dr. McFarland or Elizabeth Packard.

"Mr. Galton, why did you arrive at the conclusion that Mrs. Wilkinson was sane when she stabbed Dr. Rooney to death?" Laura was wasting no time. The question burned into the quick of the matter.

"She was part of our experiment. You mentioned my cousin, Charles Darwin. One of the first experiments I did, in 1869, was to prove that his theory that gemmules, from all the cells in the male and female bodies, circulated freely, and then combined to determine the heredity of their offspring, was false. To disprove his hypothesis, I transferred blood from rabbits of different breeds and showed there was no such transfer of characteristics. Instead, I demonstrated, once and for all, that it was the sperm and the egg which determined the hereditary ingredients of children. No psychological events or traumas that occurred during their lives ever changed their basic genetic make-up."

Clara stood up and faced the judge. "Again, how does this information support the contention of sanity in my client?"

"Please, your honor. This man is a genius. He will arrive at his conclusions momentarily. Scientific logic works as an inductive flow, not deductive, or syllogistic, as Mrs. Foltz may wish us to believe." Laura turned toward Clara and smiled.

Judge Cathcart struck his gavel hard three times upon the wood square on his desk. "Please continue, Mr. Galton. And, Mrs. Foltz. Refrain from your objections. This is not a trial. I want to hear what the gentleman has to say."

"Thank you, Judge. As I was about to say, I have studied the heredity of many famous personages, from around the world, and it is my determination that the only way to save the elite, within our Caucasian race, from being polluted and overrun by such aberrational races as the Negro and the Chinese, is to control the breeding of the female population. As we now know, the careful selection of mates is the only way to ensure the continuation of genius and the best possibilities of both mental and physical superiority. The best bred aristocrats have known and have voluntarily practiced this kind of select breeding for many generations, and they have produced the superior leaders, thinkers, athletes and warriors down through the ages. And, I might add, they also produce the best cattle, horses, sheep, dogs, and chickens."

The gallery of newspaper journalists laughed.

Clara was about to burst inside. She and her team had fought this bigoted attitude before, only to have the national government pass a bigoted law forbidding the Chinese from immigrating to the United States. As for the Negro, she believed, along with millions of other Americans, that the Civil War had decided in favor of giving full citizenship to them. But today, Negroes were still prevented from being full citizens, especially in the South. And now, this supposed genius scientist was telling everyone that the only way to ensure a perfect civilization was to control the breeding of the women? What about controlling the men?

"Mrs. Wilkinson, as you may see in her test results, is of a superior intelligence quotient. In addition, before I selected her for my experiments, I gave her a special questionnaire to determine her ability to critique possibilities between very controversial topics, such as the reasons why the male of the species has risen to be the head of a family. Granted, she completely rebelled, in some ways, saying that women needed to fight men to gain their individual freedom. However, this fighting against the patriarchy, as she termed it, demonstrated a strong will. Since she also came from the upper classes, I concluded she was quite sane." Francis Galton folded his hands and looked over at his colleague from Germany. Dr. Kraepelin returned the smile.

The rest of the presentation of the witnesses for the State was a stream of basic reinforcement of what Francis Galton had established. Mrs. Wilkinson was sane because of the I.Q. and other tests given to her by Mr. Galton. He was the expert in racial superiority and class achievement, and there was nothing Clara could say to rebut that fact. She had been silenced by both Judge Cathcart and by the metaphorical Survival of the Fittest experiment going on inside that hearing room.

When Laura called the last witness, Claiborne Falcone, Clara was almost relieved to have it concluded. Her only hope was to turn the tables during her presentation, but the odds were building against her being able to penetrate the wall of intolerant science growing all around her.

"Mr. Falcone. What were your instructions by Mr. Galton on the day Superintendent Rooney was killed?" Laura paced before her witness like a victorious cat.

"He told me that the knife I gave to her was a tin variety, quite harmless. Mr. Galton also said the experiment was to see if Mrs. Wilkinson had the male strength of character to be able to kill upon command. It was to be the final proof that she could withstand the pressures of leadership." Falcone smiled over at Clara. He was quite handsome, and Clara understood why Melissa had been so smitten by him.

"Therefore, as far as you knew, when she stabbed Dr. Rooney, she believed she was performing under your direct order and not under the authority of someone else. Is that true?"

"That's quite true. When the knife was discovered to be a real blade, I was as astonished as everyone else."

"The entire experiment, up to the moment of the homicide, was planned completely by Mr. Galton and his associates?" Laura was moving in for the kill.

"That's true. I was instructed to tell Melissa that she was helping me to escape the asylum with my brothers. We have no reason to believe any one of us could have switched the blades during the experiment." Falcone frowned. "She is quite a beautiful and trusting woman. I do not wish to harm her."

"Did you show affection for the defendant in any physically

demonstrative way?" Laura stopped pacing. She stared directly into the young man's dark eyes. "Were you not, in fact, in love with her?"

"Yes, I was. I don't see what this has to do . . ."

"Your honor. This is the most convincing evidence so far that Mrs. Wilkinson was sane when she committed this homicide. She was capable of love, and she was determined to do the bidding of her lover. I would like to call my final witness, Dr. Emil Kraepelin."

Clara was astounded. What was she doing now?

The German was sworn in, and he took the stand. Claiborne Falcone sat down.

"Dr. Kraepelin, what did you see just before Mrs. Wilkinson stabbed the victim, Dr. Rooney, in the throat?" Laura inhaled and then blew out her breath in one stream. "Take your time. If you need a translator, I can provide one."

"That is not necessary, thank you. I saw Mrs. Wilkinson rub her thumb on the blade of the weapon before she used it."

"If the court would allow. The witness has stated that he saw Mrs. Wilkinson run her thumb over the blade, to test it for strength, just before she used it. This purposeful act proves a deliberation in the mind. And, coupled with her obvious amorous affection for Mr. Falcone, she was doing it for both love and to save her lover from his prison."

Clara could hear the gasps from up in the gallery, and she knew her case was all but lost. She looked over at Dr. McFarland and Elizabeth Packard. They were frowning, with downcast stares. The presentation she would give in this hearing, no matter how eloquent or logical, was going to be a race to the bottom.

Chapter 10: The Other Experiments

The Women's Section, First Floor, Stockton State Insane Asylum, Afternoon, April 30, 1887.

It was almost a relief to Clara when they returned to the asylum to continue their investigation of the murder. Laura Gordon had been an excellent barrister. She understood the reality of the moment, she applied her direct questioning and developed her thesis. And she concluded with intelligent aplomb. However, when she met with Clara and her committee later, it was as if she were the attorney who had lost. She was downcast, hesitant in her speech, and apologetic to everyone involved with the hearing in San Francisco.

They were discussing their plans inside the committee's private room on the first floor. All were back wearing their patient attire, increasingly appearing to be actual members of the insane academy. It was Laura who made the first foray into what they should be doing to foil the plans of Francis Galton and his ambitions to create a bigoted and misogynistic paradise for the elite white class.

"I am so sorry, Clara. I had no idea this man was so filled with rancor for the working and lower classes. You know I am not in favor of any kind of class distinctions based upon racial or class privilege. I was only doing my duty as an advocate. I told the District Attorney that I will refuse to prosecute this woman in any subsequent murder trial."

Laura clasped her hands on top of Clara's as they sat together on the lower bunk. They looked as if they were two patients who had been given shock treatment. Their eyes were tearing up, their nostrils were red from crying, and the others were standing around them, trying to console and cheer them up.

"I am not depressed because I lost the hearing. I am afraid for that poor woman's life. She is now being tried for murder in the first degree, and I know that I can do nothing to protect her unless I can solve the mystery of how she was fooled into using a real blade. She has completely shut down again. She will not tell us, or anyone else, anything about what happened. How does one defend somebody who won't speak? On top of it all, we have a mental hospital that is obviously being used to promote some kind of laboratory for creating homicidal maniacs." Clara stood up and turned toward Captain Lees. "What do you think, Isaiah? I tried to show the court that what Galton was doing was inhumane cruelty. Judge Cathcart just sloughed it off as a unique way to train prospective spies for undercover military duties in the government interest."

"I know, Clara. I have faced this kind of thinking my entire career. There are those in the majority who see an encroaching take-over by the teeming masses in Asia, Africa and anywhere else where the social structure might have different values than what they see as Christian, patriotic and civilized. We have to find the murderer who is responsible for the death of Rooney, and, quite possibly, for the death of little Winnifred Cotton."

"We gave them all the statistics about the faulty diagnoses of mental illness, especially for women. Your judge was simply too impressed by this Galton to see how these insanity commitments could be caused by greed and improper procedures." Mrs. Packard put a warm hand on Clara's shoulder.

"We have to understand that we were simply outgunned inside that court room. Now we have to work harder to find corruption going on here. I agree with you, Clara. It must be part of some strange experimentation to show how poor heredity affects the brain." Dr. McFarland walked toward the door. "I'm going to question the other doctors and nurses again. Perhaps they know what's going on upstairs. Anne, please accompany me." His

119

granddaughter followed him.

"All of you. Please be careful. There is a murderer at large. I believe it is someone inside this asylum, and I will be trying to eliminate the suspects, one by one. I also need to speak with Adeline. Ah Toy, would you please inform her? I shall meet her at noon inside Jacob's Ladder. I also want to get Bertha May out of isolation." Clara walked with Isaiah out the door.

Ah Toy followed closely behind. She tapped Clara on the shoulder. "Clara, I have noticed there have been new patients being admitted. Can't we get the State to stop this until this killer is found? The more who live here, the more sheep for the wolf."

"Very good idea. I shall wire the Governor's Office immediately." Clara was the last to exit the room, so she shut and locked the door.

Later, after Clara was informed by Ah Toy that Adeline would meet her in Jacob's Ladder in one hour, she sat down inside a little nook where she could watch the passing of other patients and nurses doing their daily rounds. Both the mental patients and the nurses were obsessively compulsive. She was as well, she realized, especially when she was working on a case. She opened the folder in her hands while seated on a rickety school chair. Her number one suspect had been Dr. Rooney, until he became the victim.

As for the five hidden patients, she only got to briefly know one of them, Melissa Wilkinson, and the poor woman was now being tried for the murder of Rooney. The others were working for Galton in some kind of dastardly experiment. The Cotton parents were still on her list, and Clara had even thought about Polly being a possible killer, but now that another murder had occurred, under the direction of Francis Galton, she doubted they were involved. The final addition to her list was the lone triplet and supposed lover of Melissa Wilkinson.

Mrs. Packard told her she heard him say something quite interesting after Melissa had stabbed Dr. Rooney, but the court had not believed it related to the defendant's sanity. He said he was a Jew and that he never put the blade inside the knife Melissa used. He said they needed a martyr for their cause. Clara wondered if he could, indeed, be Jewish. Also, who was "they," to which he referred? Was it Galton and the people behind his effort to purify the white race? Somehow, she still believed this killer might be a lone assassin who had a more private motive. Why? Because if the murderer were part of this Eugenics movement, then he or she was killing the very persons this group was trying to protect. The white elite. This case was becoming more complex by the moment.

The *modus operandi*, why this killer was motivated, was the most important factor in Clara's final assessment of a suspect. Isaiah had taught her that motive also applied to criminals who were insane. The mentally ill develop purposes based on imaginary realities, but how was that really any different than what societies invent? Isn't a tribe, a society, or even a government, a type of personal creation invented by someone? This was a fact which frightened the social beings so much and comforted the loners and artists. The artists and the insane intuitively knew that the best power source for creativity came from the white hot kernel of the lonely person's mind. However, dictators and the elite knew this as well. "Therein," said Shakespeare, "lies the rub."

That brought Clara full circle. She was meeting with the one playing card in their deck who could penetrate the masculine power force now holding the asylum in check. Once they could break that binding evil, the true wisdom of what Mrs. Packard believed to be at the heart of any mind—especially the mind of the completely focused lunatic—could finally make its presence known. The lunatic is cured. The society is healed. The angels gather to help us. We need only do what Alexander Pope prescribed when he said that in order to appreciate great art, one needed to suspend one's disbelief concerning all existence.

In other words, the only Truth was that anything was possible and that change was the only common denominator. Somewhere, the killer was ready to strike again. That event, she knew, was inevitable. The murder of a child and a doctor was lurid. One needed a bold and sophisticated reason to do it. This was no spontaneous act of aggression. Clara hoped her future daughter-in-law, Adeline Quantrill, could help her uncover that solipsistic reason before death reared its ugly head once more.

***

The Women's Section, Stockton State Insane Asylum, Morning, May 1, 1887.

In four different areas of the asylum, the fictional dramas were being created. Each one had been carefully orchestrated by the research team of Francis Galton and the German visitor, Dr. Emil Kraepelin. All the required players were costumed, and the entire asylum seemed to be breathing along with the zealous jealousy and anger being developed, inside each patient, like a purple blossom of Deadly Nightshade.

Within a locked room on the second floor, Sidney Reyes was becoming a passionate damsel who was reacting to scorned love. After days of ardent love trysts with the lovely Filipina, Susanne Johansen had promised her new love a voyage back to Sweden, where they would be allowed to live together without being afraid of being locked up. Sidney believed this would change her life, and she would no longer be afraid of staying inside the cold and tortuous confines of the asylum. She sang to herself, smiled at all who passed her by, or served her needs, and she insisted that the nurses and Francis Galton call her Kitty. She was Susanne's little puss, all ready to curl her lithe young body next to her lover inside the regal family's castle in Stockholm.

Kitty was watching Susanne play the violin, the sweet strains of a Beethoven concerto wafting throughout the cold room. Attached to her identical sister, Matilda sketched them both on her pad, as they watched each other with fervent adoration. Kitty wore her navy blue patient's smock, and the sisters wore matching, green-silk evening gowns. Matilda also took sips from a blue goblet, inlaid with gold, that the new attendant, young Samuel, had brought her. Just as Susanne struck the last notes, she frowned and glanced over at her identical sister, who was, of course, attached to her body at the neck and side.

Susanne stood the varnished instrument up against the red

satin Turkish pillow, upon which they had reclined their backs, as the music was being played. Kitty watched her love bring the bow up to her lovely face and point it directly at Kitty's heaving breasts. In her mind's eye, Kitty pictured Susanne as a female matador, ready to drive the short sword into her heart at the conclusion of a bullfight.

All Kitty could see were those ice-blue eyes staring back at her. It had been this way before, on each of the days when they had met. Susanne would always point the bow at her and keep staring, until Kitty's will began to exude out of her body, like a stream of white light, and she was transformed into a mechanical doll in the P. T. Barnum Museum of Oddities. Weaving in place, Kitty was ready to do her love's bidding. Kitty danced nude, she did cartwheels, and she became a bull, rushing full-speed at the red cloth held in front of her face. Kitty Reyes was under Susanne's complete power, and now, today, was the final test.

"Look at me, Kitty. What do you see within my eyes?" The girl could see only the two eyes, and the rest of the room became a foggy blur.

"I see you, my love, for all eternity. You make me come alive once more. I am no longer a girl of the streets. I am just as noble and as artistic as you. I will do anything you ask. Just take me away from here! I cannot stand this prison that keeps us apart." Kitty was panting and flexing her fingers, unconsciously, still swaying from the rhythm of the violin, which had ceased playing. Those eyes were engulfing her entire being, until she felt them encircling her, and her body became an aperture into another dimension. It was a place where she could find solace and peace at long last. Her parents in the Philippines would be so proud of her. She had found her true calling. She was an Angel of True Love, ready to respond to the most wonderful power imaginable.

"I love you so very much, my darling! Just tell me what to do." Kitty writhed on the floor, extending her dark arms toward Susanne's glowing beacons of Aryan hope.

"I am sorry, but my sister has told me she cannot allow you to come back with us."

The words were floating out of her love's pert, crimson lips, but Kitty could not quite fathom their meaning. "She told you what?"

"You cannot be with me, my love. There is only one way. You must strangle her to death. We do not share any vital organs. I can be free of her at last. Don't you see? The doctors will slice away her useless body from me, and I will be yours forever. Please. You must. Get up, and take this scarf from me." Susanne untied the thick, mint-green scarf from around her thin waist and thrust it toward Kitty.

The mesmerized young Filipina stood up, and reached out, taking the scarf into her two hands and wrapping the ends around her fists. As she shuffled toward Matilda, she could hear the woman scream, but the sound gradually faded. It became a weak background noise inside a phantom tune. Kitty could hear only the revolutionary battle hymn of her home country, as she stood behind the screaming blonde beauty, her scarf held taught between her closed fists. The screams melded into the music, until Kitty brought the stretched silk up over Matilda's head and down around her ivory throat. Matilda tried to pull away from her sister, but she was imprisoned as always.

As Kitty twisted the material tighter, she watched Matilda's face gradually flush, and then turn crimson red. Kitty kept glancing, back and forth, between Matilda's wide "O" mouth, her silent scream of asphyxiation, and her lover's dagger-blue eyes.

"Stop! I command you to desist." Susanne was now screaming at Kitty, but the young patient did not cease her strangulation. Only when Matilda's form was slumped over, and the victim's throat was pulling on the skin between their two necks, did Kitty's wide brown eyes begin to relax. But Sidney Reyes continued to hold onto the scarf, as if her freedom were contained inside Matilda's lifeless body, which had previously been compelled by birth to be a millstone anchor. Now Matilda had been miraculously transformed into filial detritus calmly drifting upon an ocean of true love.

***

Angela Thoma was being asked to search for the spirit that was the asylum murderer. Francis Galton had entered the room to tell her what she had to do.

"Angie, I am releasing you into the patient population. Do you remember Mrs. Wilkinson?" The old Englishman pointed to the empty bunk in the middle of the room. She was the only patient in her group of five who was still inside their room on the second floor. The young Filipina had been taken in the early morning. The deranged woman who believed she was sharpshooter Annie Oakley was gone about ten minutes later. Finally, the dreamer named Jessica was escorted out by a young man named Samuel, just before Mr. Galton arrived.

Angela nodded and smiled at her caretaker. The only thing she remembered about Mrs. Wilkinson was that she used to mimic the behaviors of everybody in the room.

"The evil spirit with whom you conversed took over Mrs. Wilkinson's body. She then stabbed Dr. Rooney to death with a knife. She is now in jail facing murder charges. You were correct, Angie. The ghostly presence you heard is now wreaking havoc upon our asylum population. It can enter and possess anybody at any time. This is why I want you to go out into the population and track this entity down."

His eyes were wide with fear, and Angela could sense the foreboding in his voice. If a famous scientist like Mr. Galton believed in her, then she finally must be getting well. Perhaps, if she could find this demon, Mr. Galton might even allow her to return to her family.

"Here. Take this." The Englishman handed Angie a small Derringer pistol. "I am afraid the only way we can stop this demon spirit is to trap it inside a dead body. The released soul of the victim will kill the demon before it is released to heaven. Keep it inside your pocket. Don't show it until you have found the evil spirit, which possesses the poor body of one of our patients."

Angela felt the hard steel of the pistol, and she tucked it inside the pocket of her blue smock. She now believed she was on a mission to rid the asylum of a potential threat. If she was successful, she knew it would mean she would be released to her family.

As she passed by Mr. Galton's body, Angie could feel the heat from it. She knew that her intuitive ability to connect with the spirit world was radiating inside her once more. She felt the same powers she had whenever she searched the cemeteries, the haunted mansions, and the underground crypts with her family. It was if she had become a gigantic magnet that could sense the spirit world's presence.

This was the first time she had been allowed outside the room alone. The crane nurse had taken her to meet the unknown woman who had inspired the mystical awakening inside. She heard that voice of doom. If she could find this voice again, she knew it would be the one Mr. Galton said had possessed Mrs. Wilkinson.

All of her senses were on high alert. She could smell the perfume wafting from one of the wealthy women, who was standing near the stairs that circled from the second floor down to the main level. The woman was tall and gangling in her beautiful red gown, and she was singing an aria from *Aida*.

Angie could feel the pull from downstairs as she stood beside the insane woman. The notes from the woman's full-throated, soprano voice bathed Angie's ears like a lovely waterfall. In her mind, Angie was transforming into the young slave girl from the opera.

It was the fourth act, and she knew she must find the vault wherein the Egyptian court had sentenced her lover, Radamès, to be buried alive. As the woman sang at the top of the stairs, Radamès had refused to renounce her. Angie gently stepped down the stairs, leading her toward the lower depths of the burial vault. She knew that this demon spirit's voice was inside the same tomb where she, Aida, was supposed to die with her true love. Could it be that the same spirit that mourned for Aida and Radamès has also possessed women inside this asylum and made them kill others?

All around her, on the first floor, Angie could see the other slaves, groaning and wailing, the steel shackles on their legs dragging along the wooden, feces-stained floors. The sounds of their agony forced Angie to cover her ears with her hands. She could still search for the demon spirit with her loins, with her breasts, and with her soul.

Angie, in abject fear, lugged her body along the walls, her hands probing for a secret passage. Her ears were on alert for the sound of the demon's voice, and she pressed the right side of her face against the graffiti-adorned surface. The words of the scrawled curse seemed to penetrate into her head. *Let me out of this hell on earth!*

Her eyes were wild, as she shook her auburn tresses in exasperation. No sounds were coming to her yet. She must open her body to the passionate Devil, she must find the vibrations, the odors of extinction and lost love, the monstrous roar, and the touch of death. This voice would finally tell her that she had found the person the demon now possessed. Her freedom could be around this next corner, in another room, down another hallway.

When Angie did find the vault, and the killer's spirit, would she be able to shoot the body that held it? If this demon were possessing a human form, then the only way she could end its power over humanity would be to kill the body of the possessed. The possibility of freedom exalted her being like nothing she had ever felt before. Her fingers encircled the pistol in her pocket, and she took in a deep breath of possible salvation.

***

Earlier . . . the new assistant, who told Katherine Sue Yantis that his name was Samuel, called for her in the asylum room on the second floor. Mrs. Yantis was expecting him, as this was the day she was to rendezvous with the King of Sweden, Oscar II. On the way outside to the firing range, Samuel ushered her into a room near the kitchen.

"Please put these clothes on." Samuel pointed to the buckskin fringed skirt and matching top hanging on a clothes peg next to a barrel of molasses. Kathy quickly changed, with Samuel turning his back, and she was soon wearing the attire she knew well. When she pulled on the long black boots, with spurs, and adorned her curly-blonde head with the cowgirl hat, which was resting on the barrel, her transformation was complete. As sharpshooter Annie Oakley, her authentic identity was at last revealed.

"Mrs. Oakley! I'm so happy you have come." Madeline Olsen, King Oscar's Foreign Secretary, scampered up to Katherine, from out of the shadows of the improvised shooting range, with a Winchester rifle in hand. All four participants were standing between white chalk lines, next to the asylum's vegetable garden, which separated the waving corn stalks and green potato plants, from the rifle range's empty corridor. The shooting path extended 200 yards, ending in a straw-filled, bulls-eye target at the far end.

Katherine accepted the rifle from the secretary and thrust it above her head with both hands. "Thank you. No wind today. That's wonderful weather for my exhibition."

Francis Galton, who was looking at her from the periphery, grasped the elbow of another gentleman, who, to Katherine's limited military knowledge, looked like some sort of naval officer. He had that boat-shaped cap that curled up on the front, and those fancy gilded epaulets, streaming golden spaghetti down his shoulders. He also had a silver banner streaming across his portly chest and a silver sword and scabbard dragging from his waist. They were both heading toward her, so she believed this must be the king.

From the first moment he gazed into her eyes, she could sense his inner lust, pulsing like a sleeping tiger, just beneath his chest. Katherine knew he was going to make a move, but she did not know when. Would he wait for her to show him her marksmanship? No, one would assume not, as he had now wiggled himself over to stand next to her. She could smell the odor of sardines, a brand, which she remembered, was given the name of this horny personage now wagging his gray beard at her: King Oscar.

"How wonderful it is. In this great land, the women can protect themselves against invasion." She watched, as he brought his right hand up to his head, grasped the front of the boat hat, and swiped it upward at first, extended it in a wide arc above his head, and then, simultaneously with his bending torso, he brought that same hat cascading across the soil, until it was swept up, in another wide arc, to his head once more.

The king turned backward toward Mr. Galton and whispered frantically into his ear. Mr. Galton, smiling, stepped toward her and grasped her forearm, gently holding it, between his fingers, as if she were his prized piglet at market.

"The King would very much enjoy speaking to you, in private, before the demonstration. He wants to explain his military philosophy to you concerning snipers. Please, accompany us to my private dining area inside."

Katherine followed the two men, holding the rifle down, beginning to sense a strange presence as she walked. It was as if the asylum were calling her, and it was the first such calling she had experienced. She was going to keep her wits about her, however, as she knew these types could turn a young woman in for any insults made against their noble breeding, either by act, or by word.

"Here we are." Mr. Galton opened the door to the room, and the odor of fresh-brewed tea filled Katherine's nostrils with its steeped grandeur. She remembered mornings with Allan and the children, awakening from pleasant dreams, and her loved ones intently listening to her explain the goal of that day's haunted mansion exploration. "Please, be seated. I shall pour for you both and then be on my way."

She was seated within touching distance, and his knees were aligned toward hers, much the way she suspected a torpedo would be fixed upon a target at sea. The discomfort she felt was not unlike facing a satyr in the Elysian Fields. You knew it was going to happen, but you still believed there might be an escape plan.

"Please, won't you stand up und show me how you address a target?" The pressure inside her was mounting. Katherine's body was radiating its sonorous vibrations outward, attempting to gauge the threat of this man. However, she did as he asked and stood up.

She brought the rifle up, from parade rest, to order arms. Katherine could feel the varnished butt of the rifle's stock, and her left hand moved up to grasp the upper stock beneath the rifle's muzzle. She then moved the rifle upward, toward her cheek, to point, as a standing unit, toward the wall on the other side of the room.

She placed her right eye socket against the black scope and looked into it. From the corner of her eye, she saw that the king had disrobed. He was now standing there, his manhood exposed, smiling back at her with unabashed ardor. At least, the amorous intent was certainly making something stir beneath his stomach.

"Did you know that English composer, Edward Elgar, composed a suite for the lunatics at the Worcester County Lunatic Asylum? Everyone. The staff, the patients, they all felt wonderful after hearing the music. You are like that music to me, my sweet lady. Can't you see? My passion for you holds no bounds! Jawohl!"

Katherine was now looking at the king through the scope of the rifle. All she could hear, however, was the voice that had penetrated her consciousness again. It was the same voice that told her she was Annie Oakley and not that insane woman, Katherine Yantis. When it spoke, she could feel the tribulation it caused, up and down her spine. When she saw this man's penis, it became an onerous object, one that would keep her from her family. It took on the shape of a dagger, a weapon, and she gritted her teeth until they chattered from rage.

"What are you doing, my cooing little dove? We are playing a joke. That gun is not loaded. Come. Make an old man happy. I will reward you with anything you want. I am a doctor. A psychiatrist. I can have you released at once from this asylum. Do you want that?"

She now knew for certain. This man did not have a Swedish accent. It was German. He was an impostor and a rapist. Katherine's forefinger began to twitch around the trigger. As her gaze wandered around his body, from his balding head, to his graying chest hair, and down to that beacon of male inferiority, she heard the voice again. *Shoot him! He will not release you. He is the keeper of the crypt. Where the idiots are imprisoned. Spittle, feces, wails. Shoot him!*

After she pulled the trigger, she sniffed at the odor of the cordite, permeating the air around her, from the bullet's discharge. Her aim was off. Was it an omen of her crumbling persona? She could feel her mind splitting off, becoming other minds, other women, other emotions. A lost world, where an old man did not bleed from his arm, clutching his admiral's sleeve as if he were in control of his pulsing heart. No. He was not in control of any heart. She would always keep that control, until she, one future day, lost it, to unforeseen circumstances.

***

Earlier . . . The handsome young man she dreamed had a name. It was Samuel. He was there to escort her to meet with the other young dreamer named Polly Bedford. But first, he told her she needed to take a magic injection to allow her to see the dreams Polly created. Sarah said we all dream our own versions of reality, so why shouldn't she accept this girl's version?

After Samuel injected her, Jessica began to feel much more relaxed. When he took her hands into his, she almost floated as she stood up. She became very conscious of her eyelids. Blinking became a magical window shade to a new reality, which was burgeoning around her, second by second. The past disappeared, the future did not exist. Only the blinking moment was important, and Jessica followed Samuel out the door and into the asylum.

"Did you know, Samuel, that books are just dreams that we read. The dreamer has written their own dream down, and we can choose to view it, or not, it makes no difference, really. Only your own dream matters."

As she followed Samuel down the winding stairway, Jessica was watching her new dream world enfold around her. She decided Samuel was dreamt by her to keep her company. He seemed kind and attentive, unlike the other women around her who were preoccupied with their own dreams. Some of them were even crying and making nervous movements with their hands, faces, and legs. There was one taking off all her clothing. The other woman, in all-white, was chasing her down, picking up the articles of clothing as she ran after her.

"Will we be there soon, Samuel? These phantoms are frightening me."

"Here we are, Jessica. This is Miss Polly Bedford. Like you, she comes from San Francisco's wealthy area. Her parents had to let her rest here, just as yours allowed you to stay for your own health. Polly? This is Jessica Adkins."

Samuel guided Jessica to the chair next to where Polly was seated on the bed. Polly was drawing again on her pad. She looked up and smiled at Jessica. Dreamers meeting for the first time. Jessica was pleased.

"Why did you kill my friend?" The question was absurd. Jessica knew nothing about this girl's friends.

"I don't understand what you mean. I have never met you before now. I do not know your friends." Jessica's heart began to thrum inside her chest. She should quickly dream this girl back into some semblance of order. She was acting like another Dennis Leary.

"Deidra Watkins kept me safe. She knew how to play Mental Metamorphosis. You are from those others. The ones who would keep me from preventing their atrocities and murders. Get away from me! I want Deidra! I want Deidra!"

Jessica covered her ears. This was not her dream. This girl was insane. Her voice was ripping apart the veil between their separate dreams. Her evil nature was attacking Jessica's sedate reality. Jessica began to sweat, and she picked up a blanket from the nearby bunk and bit into it to stop a scream from erupting. She then realized it was her dream, and this girl was not meant to be inside her world. She was an intruder who needed to be silenced!

"Stop it, Jessica! You're smothering her!" Jessica felt the delicious strength of her arms holding down this girl's body on the mattress. She was squirming and flailing, but to no avail. Soon, she would disappear from Jessica's dream and vanish into her own nightmare.

Jessica Adkins was being carried, and as she looked back at the girl named Polly, who was now sitting up and breathing in deep gasps, her mind became fogged over with a peculiar notion. Dreams were forever meant to be on a collision course, and there was nothing she could do to stop it.

Chapter 11: A Killer on the Loose

The Women's Section, Jacob's Ladder, Stockton State Insane Asylum, Morning, May 1, 1887.

Clara trusted having her beau, Captain Isaiah Lees, standing guard at the bottom of Jacob's Ladder. However, when she examined their history a bit more closely, it was she who had rescued Isaiah and his partner, Eduard Vanderheiden, from an explosive situation in Chinatown. Nonetheless, the previous evening, when she had slipped out of her bunk and rendezvoused with Isaiah at this same location, his attentive display of affection smoldered her common sense out of the picture, and all she could see was his smiling face above her.

Adeline was up there in the heavens, waiting, and Clara swept the small girl into her arms and swung her about the room. It must have been the residual passion remaining from the night before. When she placed her back on Earth, Clara knew, because she was not returning her smile, that Adeline was full of important information. She could see that the girl's cheeks were flushed, even under the poor lighting, and she was breathing hard.

"Oh my, Mrs. Foltz. Something is happening today, but I have no specific locations to give you. I would not know this much but for my inter-communications with your son and my reading of Mr. Galton's mind."

Clara draped her arm around Adeline's shoulder. "Calm yourself. This is most important to our investigation. My Samuel. Is he inside the asylum? Since when?"

"Since yesterday. He told me Mr. Galton was blackmailing him. Unless Samuel did what Galton instructed, evidence would be given to the police that Polly Bedford testified seeing Samuel murder little Winnie Cotton. Galton also told Samuel that unless he complied I would never get a recommendation for the work I've done here. I don't care about that! I just want to save Samuel. I hope you can help us."

After escorting Adeline over to the two stuffed chairs, in the corner near a wall gaslight, she sat facing her. Clara wanted her mind to be as focused as possible. There could be no untoward mental errors made from this moment forward.

"Have you spoken to Bertha? Where is she and what does she know?" Clara placed her right hand on Adeline's knee and squeezed. "We have suspects now, but I want to add more information to what I have."

Adeline looked toward the ceiling, just the way she approached her channeling posture when contacting the spirit world as a medium. "She is inside a locked room on the second floor. Room 248. Only Samuel has been allowed to talk to her in his duties as Mr. Galton's personal attendant. He told me she was privy to a plan by Galton to use all five of the secret patients in his research experiments concerning heredity. He knows not about what each experiment consists. It is happening today. He does know that."

Clara squeezed Adeline's knee harder. "How does he know it's today?"

"Because he will play an integral part in what will occur."

"Be more specific. This may be the turning point in our investigation. Think carefully, and get every word correct."

"I'll try my best. Although, I do not have your eloquence or emotion. Samuel is going to escort three of these five female patients to their destinies. He did not know their names, nor how to match each name to the specific experiment. Bertha, however, did know the names and what each was going to be doing in the experiment. I was able to channel his conversation with the late Dr. Rooney while Bertha was listening inside the dumbwaiter. Samuel could not match these women to what he had been instructed to do."

"Just give me what you know. You have a photographic memory, so I know it will be quite accurate. Perhaps we can make sense of these details later."

"All right. The first woman's name is Melissa Wilkinson, but you probably know that. Of course, she is now up on murder charges. The second patient is the young Filipina, Sidney Reyes." Adeline's brow furrowed, and she stared off into space. She was channeling her memory from that moment in Francis Galton's mind. "My conjoined twins have established the necessary lustful attraction, and Susanne tells me she should soon have complete control over this Filipina's mind. In phase two, I want to see if that control can lead to murder."

"My God! You're giving me Galton's exact words." Clara was frantically scribbling notes with a stubby pencil upon her small pad. "And the third?"

"Mrs. Angela Thoma. I had my psychic assistant, Miss Quantrill, impersonate a voice from the dead to arouse this woman's sick psyche into a state of suspended disbelief. She can now easily be manipulated by this means, and the same test will be applied to her."

"How interesting. Go on." Clara was rapidly calculating possibilities as she listened. She was torn between hearing Adeline out and rushing downstairs to stop what was most certainly beginning to happen at that very moment.

"The fourth and fifth experiments are being done to Mrs. Katherine Yantis and teenager Jessica Adkins. Yantis believes she is Annie Oakley, the famous sharpshooter. Galton says his Swedish solo triplet, Deandra, shall impersonate King Oscar's personal secretary. At the rendezvous, Mrs. Yantis will be tested to determine if she can kill with a Winchester repeating rifle. As for Miss Adkins, this girl has agreed to meet with Polly Bedford. Galton has a drug he's been testing, and he shall use it on the Adkins girl. With her present psychosis, they can see how far they can extend her dream world. Hopefully, she will enter into homicidal tendencies."

Clara was flummoxed by this challenge. She knew it would be next to impossible to find out the locations of all these so-called experiments at this late hour. All she could hope to do would be to perhaps meet one of the participants during a wild goose chase. Her

Samuel was her immediate concern. She knew he was not averse to danger. He had proved that at the Winchester house in San Jose, the year before, when he charged down into the basement to stop the mercury poisoning from happening. Was he now playing along with Galton and company in order to spy for her? That sounded like him.

"Adeline. I want you to find Samuel. He knows where his sister is, and we need to get her out of that room. I want to find out where he was today and what happened. I believe it may be the last chance we have of finding the killer. I'm also sending my team out to possibly disrupt this day's events." Clara hugged the girl tightly. "You've been doing a wonderful job. We now need to move fast, so be on your way."

The older woman watched the girl dart over to the ladder stairs, reach down, and knock on the trap door three times. This was the signal to Isaiah to let her out. "Oh, and Adeline. I need to tell you one more thing."

"Yes, Mrs. Foltz?" The girl turned toward the voice.

"Don't let Galton read your mind. If he discovers what you know, he will become very suspicious. You don't need to end up in isolation, or, even worse."

"Don't worry. Mum's the word." Clara could see Adeline bring her right hand up to her closed lips and make a twisting motion, pursing her lips tightly together.

As Adeline disappeared down the Jacob's Ladder, Clara glanced around the place where she had made love the night before. Those stacks of rice in burlap bags, where she had reclined, Isaiah towering over her. The long shelf of spices where they had thrown their clothing in a mad rush to become one. She was also picturing what could happen to her children, including her newly adopted daughter, Adeline Quantrill. If Galton and his group were as powerful as she now believed them to be, they might be able to arrest her two children and Adeline, and when they uncovered the fact that they were spying for her and her committee, her entire career as a lawyer and detective would be in jeopardy.

The only chance they had would be to find the killer before he or she murdered again. This would make their efforts, even their spying, more acceptable to the public and to the authorities in the State of California. Clara had already begun a file listing the irregularities during the insanity hearing and the questionable methods being used at the asylum. Now they needed to put the pressure on before their committee's methods were discovered. It seemed she were hoping for the worst possible result, but, in effect, it was the only result that could save them.

***

The Women's Section, Stockton State Insane Asylum, Morning, May 1, 1887.

It was the job of the strong to protect the weak. This was the opposite of what was actually happening. The strong were using the poor, the insane, and the wretched of the Earth in order to establish a dictatorship above them. The wealthy, the strong, and the bigoteds were all conspiring to collect all the riches of the world and use this wealth against them.

Today was the day she had been waiting for. Satan had changed into His original form: The Redeemer Angel for All of the Earth's Downtrodden. As she lifted the mattress, she could picture it all playing out in her mind. Experiments to prove humans were nothing more than victims of their own heredity. Satan had spoken to her about Francis Galton and his work.

She must stop this madness before it took over the consciousness of the public. If Galton succeeded, many more innocents would be locked up, the keys thrown away, and never again would freedom be the vanguard for the future. Only oppression, wars, and misogyny would be accepted to stop the tide of immigrants, hungering for opportunity, needing a chance to start over, wanting to live a life away from hatred and fear. Instead, they would be sailing into a country of madness and destruction!

As she chose the first tool, the poison, she remembered how she had succeeding the time before, with the blade. Satan took it from her in a regal ceremony, in the darkness, as she stood naked and held it out to Him. She wandered while the others slept.

Even a madhouse has a skeleton key. Why would it not? It was very appropriate and kind of the lazy superintendent, Dr. Alfred Rooney. He kept it inside his office, and she had, one day, heard one of the nurses tell another nurse that she could get the drugs by using that key. It opened all the rooms inside the asylum! It was inside a drawer in the wall behind the picture of Jewish Governor Washington Bartlett. Rooney did not bother to lock it, as he was also receiving a share of the proceeds from these clandestine and profitable business transactions. The nurses and attendants who were making money selling drugs to the crazy rich women upstairs called that drawer the "Jewish hideaway."

She had also read about the plans of the experiments by using this key. Again, in the night, she read about the five experiments being planned, written on a document inside a folder on Rooney's desk. Satan had laughed gleefully when she told Him.

The entire asylum was coming alive at last. All the dead souls were being redeemed, and she could feel their jovial presence all around her, as she strolled down the halls, in the evenings. The chill that dispersed and made each room as cold as ice. This icy breathing was the anger from these souls. As every authentic Spiritualist understood: on Earth, Hell was its opposite. Heat was cold. Death was life. Insanity was sane.

Satan watched it all happen, and He told her about it later. The blade was inserted. The poison was administered. The guns were loaded with real bullets. And the hallucinogen was added to the morphine, at the last moment.

Now she could provide her Master with his tools at her leisure. She had the key, she had collected the tools, and she had the powerful will that Galton wished he had. As Satan once said in Milton's grand masterpiece, *Paradise Lost*, "For who can yet believe, though after loss, that all these puissant legions whose exile hath emptied Heav'n shall fail to re-ascend, self-raised, and repossess their native seat?"

The weak shall inherit the Earth, with the help of its grand, original Master, forever changed, forever the Redeemer of

Mankind!

***

The Women's Section, First Floor, Stockton State Insane Asylum, Afternoon, May 2, 1887.

After the murder of Matilda Johansen, the wounding of Dr. Emil Kraepelin, and the attempted murder of Polly Bedford, the police were notified by Captain Isaiah Lees. However, in a strange twist of fate, Governor Bartlett intervened, and he gave a direct order to put the Stockton State Insane Asylum on lock-down, until further notice. Isaiah was named in the Western Union telegram as the "official investigator" on the scene, and so he now had privileges that the committee had not been privy to before.

Lees could release any person being held in confinement, which meant Bertha May and Samuel were free to be interviewed, and they had been, and he could also question any staff member, including Francis Galton and his research group. Also, all of Galton's four research patients, and the remaining identical triplets, who had been present at the crime scenes, were now confined inside a locked room for questioning.

Captain Lees had assembled the key officials of the asylum inside the main dining room. Even though that meant the patients were being left unsupervised by doctors, Lees believed it to be prudent at the moment to have "all hands on deck," so to speak, to discuss possible preventative measures that could be taken.

Clara was in full agreement, as she now had enough information at her disposal to re-arrange her list of suspects and begin to narrow their priority. It was a matter of life and death, she believed. Unless Lees established a way to prevent another murder, the entire facility would be a free and open hunting ground for this killer to strike again.

At the main physicians' table, Clara sat next to Captain Lees. To her left, down the line, were Dr. Andrew McFarland, then his granddaughter, Anne, followed by Ah Toy, Elizabeth Packard, and attorney Laura Gordon. To the left of Isaiah Lees were the leading staff members of the asylum, Francis Galton, Dr. Kraepelin, Adeline Quantrill, and Samuel Cortland Foltz. The rest of the table included the four staff physicians and the head nurse, Mrs. Sarah Patterson.

Captain Lees stood up at his seat, looked up and down the table at his audience, and cleared his throat. "Thank you for coming, ladies and gentlemen. As this is an emergency, I want to quickly go over what has happened, and what measures must be taken to ensure there are no more murders committed on these premises. I have been given direct authority by the governor to take steps necessary to ensure the safety of lives, and this is where I must begin. The life of Miss Matilda Johansen has been taken, and her sister, Susanne, is now in surgery, at the Stockton City Hospital, to remove Matilda's corpse from Susanne's body. It is a dangerous procedure, and we hope to have good news in due time. As you can see, Dr. Kraepelin has been patched-up and is doing well, as the bullet passed through his bicep, and the bleeding was stopped in time."

"I want to thank the doctors for that. They saved my life," Dr. Kraepelin said, raising his left hand and pointing to his bandaged right arm.

"Now I want to discuss how we can stop this killer. Clara and I believe he or she is inside the asylum and will strike again. In order to plan a strategy, however, we have several unanswered questions for you. The first is to Mr. Galton. And I want the truth. Did you supply any of your staff with lethal weapons and poisons?"

Francis Galton stood up. His face was beet-red. "Never! My experiments were devised to simulate violence, not realize it. Somebody intervened to replace my harmless weapons with real ones. It began with Mrs. Wilkinson's blade, and it ended with the shooting of my colleague."

"At this point, we are not investigating possible corruption as a committee. We are trying to prevent another murder. Any one of us could become a target, and I want Clara to explain why." Isaiah turned to her, and Clara stood up.

"Thank you, Captain Lees. In order to clear the decks, we must have complete honesty from this point forward. I must be frank. I wanted to expose corruption inside this facility. In point of fact, the murder of Winnifred Cotton was of peripheral importance. Since I knew Francis Galton had special privacy given to him by the governor and Leland Stanford, to conduct research, I needed some way to discover what you were doing. My daughter, Bertha May Foltz, posed as patient Deidra Watkins. In addition, my son, Samuel, and his love, Adeline Quantrill, are also spying for me."

Clara thought Francis Galton would erupt, but he did not. Instead, he smiled, and said, "I knew that. As you may be aware, I have precognizant abilities, as does your Adeline." Galton looked down the row at his blonde-haired assistant and smiled. Adeline did not return the grin. "I am now being honest with you," Galton continued. "I do not want my abilities to become public, however, as it would not be favorable to my academic and research standing. However, as we are all possible murder targets, I want to help as much as I can."

Captain Lees interjected, "I must correct you. You are also suspects. Until I get more answers, everyone on your side of the table, including your patients and research assistants, are under suspicion. The main reason the governor has shut us down is because he wants us to ferret out the killer."

Galton laughed. "Oh really now? And how do you plan to do that, pray tell? Read our minds? Or perhaps you can feel our skulls to ascertain the phrenological basis of our inherited criminality?"

The other doctors at the table also joined in on the laughter.

Clara jumped when Isaiah brought his fist down hard on the table. "Silence! Let Clara speak!"

"You, Mr. Galton, may have telepathic ability, but Adeline, your young assistant can also commune with the spirit world. I am a liberal-minded woman. I am open to all possibilities. There is a real possibility that these circumstances may have a supernatural motive. I am certain you are all aware that before the science of mental health, most societies believed the inflicted person was possessed by some kind of demonic presence, or evil sprit, if you will." Clara looked over at Ah Toy. "Isn't that true, Ah Toy?"

"My culture, and many other cultures around the world,

believe this to be the case, even today." Ah Toy smiled. "Of course, exorcism requires the confinement of the person whose body has become possessed."

Again, the physicians, led by Galton, laughed.

"We are not going to go on an evil spirit chase, now are we, Mrs. Foltz? If so, then I shall have to wear my crucifix." Galton flicked his right hand at his shirt collar.

"In order to separate the phenomenal from the practical, we want to investigate further into your experiments, which took place yesterday, the day of the murder. First, I want Dr. McFarland to analyze the contents of the goblet which was seized as evidence. We need to establish the proximate cause of death. If there were a poison in Matilda's drink, then she may have died before she was strangled to death by Sidney Reyes."

"I shall do that as soon as we adjourn, Mrs. Foltz," Dr. McFarland said.

"Next, I want you to also analyze what was in the injection given to Jessica Adkins before she visited patient Polly Bedford. Perhaps Anne can do that?"

Anne McFarland raised her hand. "By all means! My grandfather and I will have the results to you shortly."

Clara smiled. "Good. As for the exchange of weapons in the experiments with Melissa Wilkinson and Katherine Yantis, we are searching for other weapons and ammunition inside this asylum that can match the ones used during the experiments. Finally, we have the fifth, and final experiment. Mrs. Angela Thoma was one of your patients, correct, Mr. Galton?"

"Yes, she was," Galton said.

"Where is she at this moment? We have been unable to locate her, and we've searched everywhere in this building and even outside. Also, we know that she was to also attempt a murder, as Adeline informed us of that fact. How was Mrs. Thoma going to accomplish this?"

"Very well. I gave her a Derringer. It was, of course, unloaded. I simply wanted her to attempt to kill a person she believed was possessed by a demon. I wanted to prove that hereditary homicidal impulses were linked to superstitious beliefs," Galton said.

Clara was furious. "And so, now that we understand there have been at least two purposeful switches made to arm weapons, there is presently a mad woman roaming somewhere inside this asylum with, most likely, another loaded gun?"

Galton was indignant. "I'm afraid I don't know who could have made those switches, and I am also unable to keep track of the hundreds of patients living here. I have been contracted by the State and Leland Stanford to do research, not to be an asylum supervisor. The former superintendent has been murdered, as you know, and there has been no replacement made."

"Your research, as of this moment, has been suspended, Mr. Galton. We now know, thanks to your staff, that there is an armory, of sorts, in one of the store rooms, and we shall be searching it for possible bullets that could have been used in the experiments. Until we complete our investigations, nobody will be armed." Clara's voice was adamant.

"What? Are we supposed to roam these halls without any bloody protection?" Galton and the asylum doctors stood up, and they were all livid.

"Captain Lees will be the only person with a weapon. The only weapon we know that is out there is the single-shot Derringer in the possession of a madwoman, Mrs. Angela Thoma. Let's be on the look-out for her, shall we? I also need a key to the weapon storage room. Since each door seems to have its own key, is there perhaps a master key Captain Lees can use?"

Clara watched as the head nurse, Sarah Patterson, raised her hand. She was frowning, and Clara nodded at her to speak.

"I'm afraid it's been stolen. It was kept in a wall drawer in Dr. Rooney's office. Behind the painting of Governor Bartlett. I went to retrieve it this morning, and it was gone."

It was Isaiah's turn to be livid. "What? You kept a skeleton key for an insane asylum? Now, not only might we have a murderer on the loose, he or she could also have access to every room in this house!"

Clara turned to her beau, and her voice was placating. "This answers a lot of our other questions, Captain Lees. We need to speak of it in private."

Captain Lees gravely nodded, but he was still glowering at the head nurse.

As Clara watched the asylum staff file out of the dining room, she ran over to Adeline and grabbed her arm. "Adeline, stay a moment. You, too, Samuel. I want to ask you some more questions. I may be able to narrow my suspect list down to two people, if I can get the correct answers from you."

Chapter 12: Everyone Can Dance

The Women's Section, First Floor, Stockton State Insane Asylum, Afternoon, May 2, 1887.

Clara wanted to ask Adeline and Samuel about two events they must have witnessed. She also needed to question Adeline's vast mental reserve of knowledge. First, however, she hugged them both closely to her. She then sighed.

"You have been magnificent! I wanted you to know that before I ask you these questions. I wish Bertha were also with us, but you can tell her. First, I know that Samuel accompanied Miss Jessica Adkins when she visited Polly Bedford on the first floor. What exactly happened when you were there?"

Her twenty-year-old was visibly concerned. He kept running his hand through his dark hair as he spoke. "They seemed to be getting on quite well, at first. Then, for no reason that I could ascertain, Miss Adkins picked up a blanket from one of the bunkbeds and began to smother the young girl. I had to pull her off, or she would have, most certainly, killed Polly."

"Can you remember what they said? It's very important. We'll soon be getting the analysis of what was in that injection you gave her, but I need to know exactly what might have been stated to instigate the violence." Clara reached out and held Samuel's hand.

Samuel's eyebrows furrowed in concentration. "Let me see. Just before Jessica attacked her, Polly accused her of killing somebody. Her friend. But she didn't say who it was."

"Perhaps she meant Winnifred Cotton. Go on." Clara's mind was working, making connections.

"Polly then told Jessica she wanted Bertha, or Deidra, to come back to her. She said Deidra played a game with her. I think she called it Mental or Mind Metamorphosis. When she began to scream Deidra's name, Jessica grabbed the blanket and attempted to smother her."

"Thank you. Now, Adeline. How did Polly identify the murderer when she spoke with Bertha that day when we were back at the Hopkins' mansion in San Francisco? What exactly did she call him?" Clara wanted to pinpoint the language used.

Adeline stared off into space. She was channeling the past. "Bertha first stated this, 'It's time to use your mental metamorphosis. If you become his mind, as he is in the act of killing a girl, tell me what you would be thinking and how you could change the reality of murder into something worthwhile and even redeeming.' Polly told her the killer of Winnie Cotton was a demon of some kind. And then, when Bertha had chided her for believing in ghosts, Polly described him thus, 'You would pray there were ghosts, because no human could stop him. When he turned toward me, I saw his face was a continually changing compendium of different people's faces. I fantasized under stress about the possible reasons for this to occur. I may have eaten something horrid or poisonous. Or, supernaturally, I may have been put under a curse of some kind. Could I be an enemy of the government, who needed to be disposed of?' Is this what you wanted, Mrs. Foltz?"

Clara smiled. "Yes. That's exactly what I wanted. You may both leave. Samuel, I want you to hunt for Polly Bedford. Bring the girl to me at once. Also, at five tonight, after dinner, I want you and Bertha to stay with us inside our room. I'll have the staff put in two more bunk beds. I then shall explain to everyone what I believe we now face."

After the children left, Clara summarized what she now had in the way of suspects. Her list had begun with ten. Now, after all that had occurred, she believed there were only two possible murderers. The Cotton parents were out of the picture, as was Leland Stanford. However, since the Cottons were the elite class that Stanford and Galton had vowed to protect, the murder of little

Winnifred demonstrated that the murderer was trying to penetrate that exclusive club of genetically superior white families. The killing of the very elite Scandinavian socialite, Matilda Johansen, and the murder of wealthy Superintendent and Eugenics supporter, Dr. Alfred Rooney, proved her theory. Then, when Dr. Emil Kraepelin was shot, and Polly Bedford herself became a target, Clara realized how insane the girl really was.

Polly Bedford believed she was in league with some kind of superior, supernatural entity who would save humanity from those who enslaved lunatics and women. She had staged her own murder, at the hands of Jessica Adkins, in order to trick Clara and her committee. And, now that Clara knew what Polly Bedford had stated, to Bertha, about what the killer looked like, the attorney had reached her conclusion.

The only suspect of the five of Galton's patients who tried to murder Polly Bedford was Jessica Adkins. Now that Clara knew the insane Jessica had been drugged, that meant she was no longer a suspect. Jessica, like the other patients and assistants of Francis Galton, did not have access to the rest of the asylum, especially the downstairs and main storerooms where the armaments and pharmaceuticals were stored. That meant that Claiborne Falcon, whom she suspected might be a Jew, was not a suspect. He and the other identical triplets had not come downstairs at any time. Superintendent Rooney's office was downstairs, and that was the location of the missing master key. That left twelve-year-old daughter of their wealthy neighbors, Polly Bedford.

Clara knew that Polly had described the killer as someone who had tried to cut Winnifred Cotton with a blade of some kind. This person was trying to stop the girl from breeding, so that meant sterilization. At first, Clara had thought Francis Galton and Leland Stanford might be behind such activities. Now, however, Clara understood the logic behind the mad girl's statement. She was attempting to show that the elite were not superior. No, in fact, Polly Bedford, the insane child genius, was trying to discredit and stop Stanford and Galton's effort to incarcerate lunatics by showing that the elite class could be just as vulnerable to evil as any other class.

Clara knew she could not allow this information to be disseminated to the press or even to Polly's family. She also believed that Polly was going to strike again, as she now had the master key to all of the rooms and hidden rooms of this asylum. Clara needed to explain what she believed was going to occur tonight inside the asylum, but she first wanted to hear from Samuel.

As she looked around the vacant dining room, Clara could sense the same ominous presence she had felt on the first day she crossed the threshold of the Stockton State Insane Asylum and heard a woman scream within. When her son burst through the door, she knew.

"She's missing, mother. Polly Bedford cannot be found anywhere," he told her, his chest heaving from running around the asylum.

The Women's Section, First Floor, Stockton State Insane Asylum, Evening, May 2, 1887.

Clara was inside the committee's private room seated on the lower bed. She wanted to tell her group what had occurred and how they needed to proceed. Nobody was missing, thank God, and the three youngsters were also there from upstairs. Two new bunkbeds had been brought in for their new residents, and, except for Samuel, Adeline, and Captain Lees, they all wore their patient's attire of navy blue pullovers. Each person was seated on his or her bed, like children awaiting a bedtime story. Clara knew this would be a grim fairy-tale, and she wanted to unravel it as carefully and logically as she could.

Dr. McFarland and his granddaughter, Anne, had accomplished their analysis of the contents in the goblet and syringe, and Clara's suspicions had been confirmed. She now needed to report the news to her comrades.

"I am very sad to report to you that our killer is a child. Miss Polly Bedford is the only suspect who could have accomplished the switches necessary to cause the violence we now know occurred. The master key to all the rooms has been stolen by her, and this was how she was able to procure the bullets, poison, and drugs she needed." Clara nodded at Samuel, who was on the upper bed near the wall. "Samuel, you became her delivery boy for these items. Matilda Johansen drank from the goblet of the strychnine-poisoned tea that killed her before Sidney Reyes attempted to strangle her. Mrs. Yantis's Winchester was also armed when you escorted her outside to the shooting range, resulting in the wounding of Dr. Kraepelin. Our other missing patient, Angela Thoma, we must assume, also has a loaded Derringer at her disposal. Finally, the injection you gave to Jessica Adkins was a concoction of both morphine and a hallucinogen. Dr. McFarland, would you like to explain the source of the administered drug and what you both have discovered?"

Dr. McFarland was on the bottom bunk and his granddaughter on the top. "When I analyzed the residual contents of the goblet given to Matilda Johansen by Samuel, I discovered that it had also been laced with the hallucinogen of peyote. Working upon an intuitive guess, I learned from Anne that the injection given to Miss Adkins consisted of liquid peyote as well, in its entirety."

Anne McFarland nodded, "Indeed it was. We were so surprised by this that we decided to check this morning's rounds of injections to be made to patients in the Women's Section. Lo and behold, every woman had been given an injection of liquid peyote. This had not occurred on previous days, so we wanted to tell you about it."

Clara was also surprised. "Do you think our Polly did this? If so, why?"

Dr. McFarland cleared his throat. "You are the detective. I do know how this drug has been used by our Native American tribes. For example, just recently, it was discovered that the nations of the Kiowa and Cherokee began using peyote in a ritualized dance called The Ghost Dance. When the European immigrants began killing their members by the thousands, the tribal medicine men, or shamans, believed their hallucinogenic dance would stop the aggression and give their warriors special powers of bravery against the maniacal onslaught of the invaders. And thus, all of the braves would also ingest the drug before going out to battle. As we know, it did not stop the slaughter."

Clara suddenly noticed that Mrs. Packard was not sitting on her reinforced bed. "Has anybody seen Liz?"

"She told me she wanted to search for Polly Bedford," Adeline said. "She said she believed she knew how to cure the child's type of mental illness. I thought you knew."

"I did not! I told all of you in the dining room this morning that I wanted you here at five. She must have not had her hearing trumpet. We now have an old woman out there in an asylum filled with hallucinating mental patients. We must find her before she gets harmed." Clara stood up and rushed over to the door. It was still locked. "Who has the key, dammit?"

Captain Lees walked over to her. He held out the room key. "As the only security officer in this establishment, I have procured all the keys. Except, of course, for the one that matters. The master key, which is now in the possession of our young murderer."

"I don't care about that now." Clara took the key and inserted it into the lock, turned it, and then pushed down on the door latch. As soon as she swung the door open, an ominous sound filled her with dread. Outside the asylum, a raging storm was beginning, and Clara could see the flash of lightening criss-cross along the wall in a dazzling and jagged display of white light, followed immediately by a tremendous boom of thunder, which shook the asylum's foundations. At the other end of the hall, she spotted the ghostly figure of a tall woman in an evening gown. She was singing an operatic aria. Clara listened carefully. It was from *Aida*. The wealthy patients from upstairs were now downstairs.

All the others joined Clara out in the hallway. The rain was pelting the tall windows in sheets, and the lightening and thunder continued, as they walked down the passageway. Isaiah had taken out his Colt-45 revolver, and he was now in front of Clara, leading the way. The gaslights flickered on the walls, and then they went out, leaving the lightening as their sole source of illumination. Clara felt a hand at her elbow. She turned, and it was her best friend, Ah Toy.

"Please. Talk to Adeline. I have some precognition, and I feel we are entering into a confrontation we are powerless to stop."

As they made their way slowly down the hallway, the lightening continuing to flash every few minutes, Clara saw other well-dressed women appearing from rooms along the way, their eyes glowing, as if the lightening had ignited something within their minds. The opera singer kept up her aria, and as they all entered the large dining room, what they saw inside was out of some macabre nightmare.

All the tables had been pushed against the walls. The piano was where the doctors' table used to be, and, between flashes of lightening, Clara observed all the twirling couples out in the middle of the floor. The piano player was one of the well-dressed wealthy women, and she was playing a robust waltz by Strauss. Hundreds of the insane asylum women were dancing, as a group of them had raided the men's section of the asylum and had brought over some dancing hostages. It was clear to Clara, however, that they were all enjoying themselves. The identical Falcone triplets were dancing also, doing pirouettes with wealthy lunatics from the second floor.

The entire staff of seventeen nurses and four doctors were tied-up with rope and gagged with kerchiefs, squirming like worms, piled up in the corner. However, on the riser, where the doctors' table used to sit, Clara saw Francis Galton and his German cohort, Dr. Emil Kraepelin. They were also tied up, standing, their hands behind their backs, but they had no gags. The other five women on the riser each had a weapon. Two of them Clara knew. Liz Packard and Polly Bedford. Mrs. Packard held her ear trumpet against her ear, the better to listen to the music, Clara supposed.

The other three must have been the patients who served as the victims of Francis Galton's experiments. One woman, dressed in fringed buckskin and wearing a cowgirl hat, was pointing her rifle at Mr. Galton. Another female, a shorter Asian, was holding a pistol against Dr. Kraepelin's side. The last woman, the teenager, Jessica Adkins, also had a pistol, which was pointed directly at Captain Lees.

Clara stepped forward. "Stop playing that music!" Clara

shouted. The piano player stopped playing, and the dancers became immobile out on the floor, turning as one toward the main riser. There was a dead silence in the dining room as they all listened. "Liz, what happened here? You do realize that Polly is the murderer, don't you?"

The former Illinois asylum resident stepped forward. She looked comfortable in her asylum uniform. She then turned toward Galton and the German and pointed her right index finger at them. "I know you must be an excellent detective, Clara, but I beg to differ. These two men are the murderers. Not only are they responsible for the deaths of Winnifred Cotton, Dr. Rooney, and the attempted murder of one of their own, Dr. Kraepelin, they were also planning to blame it all on Polly Bedford."

"This woman belongs in this madhouse! She instigated this rebellion, and if you don't believe me, ask the doctors and nurses who are gagged over there." It was Francis Galton's turn to point over to the writhing bodies in the corner.

"I must say, Liz, you need to offer us a bit more evidence than finger-pointing. What did you find out?" Clara walked closer to the riser, but when the cowgirl pointed her Winchester and cocked it, she stopped. "Your proof had better be quite good."

"While you were all doing your snooping, I spent each day talking to Polly, and I soon realized she was not suffering from a normal type of depression or obsessive fantasy. I had seen this type of behavior before, but the person who exhibited it was under the influence of a drug." Mrs. Packard pointed toward the girl. "I decided to observe the evening rounds of the doctors, and I saw them giving injections to Polly that were not on the scheduled chart."

Clara again stepped forward, and Mrs. Buckskin pointed at Clara's head. "We know, Liz. Anne McFarland analyzed the contents of the syringe given to Jessica Adkins. It had liquid peyote mixed with the morphine. And the goblet that Matilda Johansen drank also had peyote included with the poison. Polly Bedford was the only person who had access to the poison, drugs and weapons. She stole the master key from Rooney's office. She delivered them all, did she not?"

It was Polly's turn to step forward. "Indeed it was me, Mrs. Foltz. But I was not in my right mind. Mrs. Packard explained to me how they were doing it. They had been drugging me all along. Even before I was committed to this asylum."

"But why? It makes no earthly sense." Laura Gordon's attorney logic was entering the fray. "The Bedford parents of Polly are on the state's health committee. If Mr. Galton was attempting to seek favor to conduct business, then blaming their daughter for murder would not endear them to him."

"I think I have that scoundrel figured out." Captain Lees holstered his pistol. "If he can control a genius child of the elite, then he could move up. Why not the governor's child? Even the president himself?"

"Right. That's his philosophy. I read about it in the New York magazine. Only the white folks who have the best genes deserve to rule the roost." Dr. McFarland chimed in.

"Wasn't it also because they feared strong women? Perhaps women very similar to my mother." Samuel sidled his way through the dancers to the front of the room near the riser.

Mr. Galton was fuming. "You people have no concept of what it's like to face nature on its own terms. To survive and to serve are the shared rules between humanity and the animal kingdom. I have simply understood my cousin's rules and accepted them. My insight is that there are the same survival of the fittest rules in both the human and animal cultures. The racial statistics are available to rational calculators. The tribal societies were backward, and the races within those societies were brown, yellow and black skinned. The Northern European races, on the other hand, grew stronger racially because of their advanced weapons and tools, which moved them faster along the technological pathway, so they were able to subjugate the less educated and weaker tribal societies. The whites advanced faster because they were genetically superior. They were only coincidentally white. Color had nothing to do with it."

"I am sorry. I still don't understand how Polly's parents are part of this scheme, if that's what it was." Clara was beginning to believe Elizabeth's theory, but she wanted more hard evidence.

"How was having a child, who does what Polly supposedly did, a good thing for the racial elite, into which category the Bedfords certainly fit?"

"Galton and Rooney wanted the public, especially the wealthy public, to fear the possibility of racial contamination. Let me bring out the final piece of our little puzzle. Don't worry. Polly and I have discovered that all of this was written down by Galton and Rooney. We have these incriminating documents stored inside Jacob's Ladder." Mrs. Packard motioned to the buckskin woman. The lady stepped down off the riser, Winchester in hand, and walked out of the dining room.

"Clara. If Liz has all this evidence, then we can convict. We can stop this insanity before he can use it inside other asylums," Laura pointed out.

Adeline Quantrill was becoming agitated. Clara noticed her face getting that far-away look once more. This meant she was either telepathically sending or receiving. "Adeline? What information do you have for us?"

The girl stepped forward and took Samuel by his arm. "Mr. Galton has a back-up plan. I couldn't ascertain the details, but he is confident you will fail."

"Look!" Samuel was pointing at the man being escorted, at rifle point, into the dining hall. The buckskin woman was smiling, as if she had captured some wild Indian, who had been intent upon raiding their wagon train on the prairie.

The young man she was pushing toward them was, indeed, dark-skinned, with long, stringy-black hair, multi-colored beads encircling his red shirt, and a red bandana around his forehead. He also wore animal-skin moccasins.

"He looks like Navaho to me," Dr. McFarland pointed out.

"No. He's an Apache. A bit feistier. Galton's people wanted the maximum threat factor for their plan." Mrs. Packard walked over to the young native and stood beside him. "His name is Jacob Windwalker. Since his kind, as well as the Negroes and Chinese, are not allowed to be housed in exclusive insane asylums, like this, Galton and his international cohorts wanted a way to sell their grand plan to governments around the world."

Clara was astounded. "Grand plan? What is that? Certainly you don't mean . . ." The idea that was beginning to fill her consciousness was too horrible to believe.

"Yes, they were going to impregnate Polly after she menstruated. This was their method of showing the elites what would happen if the races became mixed. For, you see, Mrs. Bedford comes from native stock. When Louise Bedford's Sister, Jeanne Forester, overheard Louise tell her husband that Polly could not be interviewed by the police, she was afraid the police would inquire into the family's hereditary lineage. They attempted to cover up Polly's heritage, but I did some fact checking when I saw Polly was being drugged. When you were in San Francisco with the Wilkinson insanity hearing, I journeyed to the Stockton City Hall of Records. Louise Bedford and her husband, Ronald, came to California during the 1850s Gold Rush. Ronald, a prospector, had first met his wife in Kansas. She was a teenage orphan who had been living in a Catholic orphanage. Louise Bedford's mother was a Cheyenne squaw, one of the wives of a Dog Soldier chief named Morning Star. Louise Bedford's mother was captured by a Frenchman who had raided the village, along with his Chippewa allies, and they kidnapped Louise's mother. She was impregnated by the Frenchman, out of wedlock, and Louise was given up for adoption to the Catholic charities."

Dr. McFarland was intrigued. "I know that tribe. The Cheyenne were fierce warriors who were originally peaceful farmers in the Sheyenne River valley. They were forced out by the French into Colorado and Kansas, where they became wandering buffalo hunters. Of course, when the railroads came, the buffalo were shot from those trains, and soon, their herds diminished, until tribes like the Cheyenne had to fight for their survival as a culture."

"That's all very well and good. However, as we now know, people such as Galton and Rooney, and their adherents, have no time for tribal pity. To them, these people are all savages who needed taming and civilization to make them acceptable. The same way we treated the Negros and then the Chinese." Mrs. Packard turned to the young brave. "The Apache tribe is still detested by most settlers in California and Arizona. They raided white wagon trains and towns more than any other tribe. Galton believed when Polly became impregnated by an Apache brave, then our American citizenry would be so shocked that Galton's plans to sterilize women would be accepted more readily."

"Sterilize? How do you know this?" Clara's mind was reeling.

"Yes, it's all written down in their document, in black and white. Come with me. I want to show you something, Clara." Mrs. Packard took Clara's hand. The older woman guided her, along with Polly Bedford, out toward the exit.

"Mother! Be careful." Samuel cried.

"We'll be back shortly," Clara told him, following closely behind the two into the dark hallway.

Liz and Polly still had their pistols, so Clara felt a bit safer. The lightening and thunder cracked, sending a chill down Clara's spine. She had no idea where they were headed, but she had finally begun to realize what Mrs. Packard had uncovered. Clara had been much too conservative with her detection. It had taken a woman who was more experienced with drugs, and the ways of mental asylums, to uncover the final truth.

Clara felt something dripping on her head. She looked up, and it was the ceiling that was fissured and sending down the droplets from the rainstorm outside. Polly and Liz had stopped in the hallway near the Jacob's Ladder access. However, instead of pulling down on the cord to release the ladder up into the storeroom, Polly reached down and pulled away the Persian rug that covered the floor near Dr. Rooney's office. Beneath, as the lightening struck to reveal it, was a metal door. Polly pulled up on a lever inside the door, and it clicked. Grunting, the girl pulled the metal door upward, exposing another set of stairs, going down instead of up.

"Come, Mrs. Foltz. They're down here." Polly scampered down the stairs, as she had obviously done this before. However, Clara saw that it was pitch-dark down those stairs, and she hesitated. As she was about to tell Liz she was not going down there, two wax candles flew up from the darkness and landed at Clara's feet.

"Here are some wooden matches, Clara," Liz said, handing her the box of Indian Chief Fuzees.

Clara lit both candles, and handed one to Mrs. Packard. She followed the old woman as she carefully descended the stairs. The odor of sweat and mould hit Clara immediately, and she could hear the drips from the rain entering this cellar from above.

"Close the hatch, please," Liz told her, and Clara did so. The metal door shut with a thump.

As their candles flickered in the dampness, Clara followed, and her senses were on high alert. In the distance she could hear the sound of human beings. They were groaning and weeping. When they were finally in front of the metal cage, what Clara then saw would haunt her the rest of her life.

Clara, Polly and Liz held their candles up to the cage, and, huddled inside, there must have been fifty or some-odd women, of all ages, races and physical handicaps. Most were dark-skinned, but a few were white, speaking in different foreign languages. Like the lunatics she had met during her stay inside the asylum, they each had a lonely soliloquy, meant to satisfy their inner natures.

However, Clara noted, almost every one of these women was a physical monstrosity. Some had hunchbacks that burst out of their navy blue uniforms at strange angles, exposing wrinkled bumps, bruises, and hair patches on their discolored skin. Others had pointed heads and were bald; some had the oval, slant-eyed appearance of Mongoloids; and still others were obviously blind, with darting, bloodshot eyes that could not fix upon anything in front of them.

"This is the first group they were going to sterilize. The deformed immigrants, Natives, and Negroes. Galton believed he would gain wide sympathy from the public after he explained why he was doing this, and how much it would save the public coffers." Mrs. Packard's voice was bitter with invective. "I have seen these types of patients before. They require much more care and civility than those upstairs. They can be rehabilitated, however, and some can even perform basic chores and other tasks. The idea that

157

humans, of any physical or mental disability, should be dehumanized with the stigma of permanent sterility, is repugnant to me."

"I understand, Liz. We have other methods to keep these women chaste. If they can be rehabilitated, then why shouldn't they even have the right to procreate? From what I have studied, and from what my daughters, Trella and Bertha, have discovered in their biology courses, hereditary traits are not always passed directly from the parents. Very healthy and normal traits can come from many generations before, sometimes hundreds of years before." Clara pulled her hand back, as one of the women inside attempted to reach her hand through the bars to snuff out the candle.

Mrs. Packard's groan mixed with the imprisoned groans inside the cage. "Galton's theories have no such logic. Mental and physical abnormalities are an anathema to a bigoted person's way of seeing the world. I have fought his kind of thinking my entire life. Like my husband's way of thinking, these bigots have a fixed, incontrovertible rationale, which has no room for more reasonable approaches. They are always looking for the methods which can reap the greatest monetary wealth and a psychologically intimidating power over others. It has always been this way, and it will probably always be this way, unless we can show the public that these very real problems can be handled much differently."

From above them, there was an explosive eruption. It was not the sound of thunder, Clara realized. It was the horrendous ebullition of some kind of bomb going off outside their cellar confines. Polly Bedford was the first to run down the passageway to the stairs, followed by Clara, and, moving much more slowly, Mrs. Packard.

***

Laura, Adeline, and Ah Toy were standing beneath what remained of the Jacob's Ladder storeroom. Burnt paper, splintered wood, and ceiling wax were littered all over the first floor hallway, and there was a gigantic, jagged hole, of about twenty-five feet, directly above them, where the stairs used to be. However, all of the

158

assembled crowd, of about fifteen patients, were looking down at the mangled body of a person lying, burned and bloodied, within the rubble.

"Isaiah? What happened?" Clara screamed.

Lees had his gun out, pointed at Francis Galton and Dr. Emil Kraepelin. "It was Mrs. Angela Thoma. She found the entrance to the stairs, and she went up. This woman, who was singing an aria from *Aida* in the hallway, said she saw Angela before she climbed up into the second floor hideaway.

"Before she went up, she told me there was an evil spirit up there. She said she needed to kill it to preserve nature's purity." The tall singer began to sob, her shredded evening gown singed black from the explosion.

Captain Lees exhaled. "Galton planted the explosive device up there to protect his written plans. That was his back-up plan. Mrs. Thoma shot at what she perhaps believed to be an evil spirit, and the bomb was triggered. I'm afraid that all of the written evidence of Galton's master plan has been destroyed."

Chapter 13: Return to Sanity

The Hopkins Mansion, One Nob Hill, San Francisco, May 4, 1887.

Clara had assembled her group inside the usual meeting place, Mrs. Hopkins' Library. She wanted to explain the aftermath of what occurred during their internment at the Stockton State Insane Asylum. She also wanted to give a sort of bon voyage celebration for Mrs. Elizabeth Ware Packard, who was going on a cruise to Europe, where she would speak to mental health experts in a Paris meeting. Clara believed the ramifications of the California investigation would be changing how patients are treated, but she was also realistic enough to understand these changes would not, most likely, last very long.

As she gazed on either side of the long mahogany table at her guests and family, Clara was thinking about how wonderful it was that her detective business was becoming much more of a cooperative affair. If it had not been for having Mrs. Packard, Dr. McFarland, and his granddaughter, Anne, working along with her usual group of family members, the Stockton Asylum case would have turned out quite differently for all involved. As it was, a freak accident, a "mental metamorphosis," if you will, had changed everything at the last moment. Life was not, sadly, a game that girls played to occupy their minds. No, it was a much more serious affair that allowed obvious scoundrels, like Mr. Francis Galton, to get away, due to circumstance beyond their control.

There were ten of her friends and family at the table, the same number of people who had been on her initial list of suspects in the murder of Winnifred Cotton. To her left, Isaiah Lees sat, his usual, contemplative scowl decorating his handsome face.

Whenever she stared hard at him, however, he would look up and give her the smile reserved only for her. Next to him was Dr. Andrew McFarland, and then his granddaughter, Anne. The final three on that side of the table were family members, Adeline Quantrill, who was now officially engaged to her betrothed son, Samuel Cortland, who was beside her. Bertha May, alias Deidra Watkins, was the last person on the end.

On Clara's right were Mrs. Packard, Ah Toy, her best friend, attorney Laura de Force Gordon, Trella Evelyn, and Mrs. Mary Hopkins, the demented, but loving, head of the household. Clara had a surprise for all of them. She waved at her youngest son, David Milton, who knew to bring in the guests, who were waiting in the mansion's foyer.

One by one, each of the five guests entered the Library, and they each sat at the five chairs, two on one side, three on the other, of the long table. Clara's group watched them be seated, and there were smiles on their faces to greet them.

"Ladies and gentlemen. Let me introduce our guests of honor. On our left, Mrs. Melissa "Pepper" Wilkinson, recently discharged from the San Francisco Women's House of Criminal Detention, a free woman. Melissa is also seeing another former patient from Scotland, Mr. Claiborne Falcone, who was able to overcome his own delusion that he was a Jew. Next to her is Mrs. Katherine Yantis. Please notice that Kathy is not wearing her buckskin, as she no longer believes she is Mrs. Annie Oakley, thanks to Liz Packard's counseling. On the right, we have Miss Sidney "Kitty" Reyes, who is now attending the University of California, at Berkeley, majoring in International Studies. Next, we have young Miss Jessica Adkins, who is still an out-patient, but her mental health is improving nicely due to Mrs. Packard's counsel and the promised letters that she will receive from our chief experts here, including Dr. McFarland, myself, and Anne McFarland. Finally, we have young Miss Polly Bedford, who is now free from any mental problems, as she had been drugged most of the time by asylum officials. Please, applaud now, as we shall be adjourning to the dining room for a nice repast with my parents after this meeting."

Clara clapped her hands, along with all the others, and their five guests beamed with embarrassment.

"As you may know, our foray into the abyss that was the Stockton Insane Asylum has ended. We were not able to prosecute all the parties involved in the drug sales and experiments being done at the behest of Leland Stanford, and his new private university, but we were able to give enough hard evidence to the courts in order to release Mrs. Wilkinson and to banish Francis Galton and Dr. Emil Kraepelin back to Great Britain and Germany. Since we could show that Melissa Wilkinson had no knowledge that the weapon she was using was provided from the asylum's armory, she was, therefore, not responsible. In addition, since the person who was murdered, Dr. Alfred Rooney, had ordered the drugging of all patients with the hallucinogen, liquid peyote, Mrs. Wilkinson was not in her right mind at the time of the stabbing. Pepper, would you like to add to what I have just said?" Clara nodded over at the bright-eyed woman wearing a robin's egg blue spring frock.

"I know. I seem to have my speech back. My family now believes I should have it turned back off. However, thanks to Mrs. Foltz, and, most especially to Mrs. Elizabeth Packard, I have my normal wits about me today. After having learned that there are groups wherein I can voice my displeasure with the patriarchal system that is today ravaging female and immigrant rights, I have a normal outlet for my pent-up grievances. We are growing in numbers, every day, and with people like you behind our efforts, I dare say, we shall be victorious!"

"Thank you, Pepper. Your invigoration is very welcome in our Suffrage Movement, and your nickname is well applied, in moderation, of course. I also trust my lawyer friend, Mrs. Gordon, is now aware of how drugs can affect the mental state of a homicidal perpetrator." Clara glanced at Laura, and she was pleased when her friend nodded her head in agreement.

"Mother, how did you not miss the fact that Polly's parents were trying to hide the information that her mother Louisa's side of the family was from native heritage? You need only have contacted me in San Francisco to do such research." Trella Evelyn, ever

Clara's antagonist, was again prompting a debate.

"I made a mistake. I have no excuse, other than the fact that we were hard-pressed for time at that moment. Thankfully, however, I had appointed a woman who had such experience, and who filled in for you very nicely. I know, Mrs. Packard and I are not from your generation, Trella, but we do attempt to keep up." Clara smiled at her eldest daughter, and Trella smirked.

"What do you suppose was in that master plan of Francis Galton's? If we had been able to use that as evidence, I dare say, there would be nothing left of this Eugenics controversy," Dr. McFarland pointed out.

"I know. I would assume it was filled with the same bigoted and misogynist declarations that he made in court. Now that the public is aware of the sterilizations he was planning, they are quite angry, especially our suffragists. One would hope our populace is educated enough to see through such bigoted logic, but only time and history will tell," said Clara.

"I want to know, how did Mrs. Packard enlist the aid of the entire community of patients in order to rebel against Galton and his staff?" Anne McFarland asked.

Clara noticed that Liz Packard was not using her ear trumpet. So, she pointed at it, as it was lying in front of the older woman's place at the table. Liz nodded and picked it up, placing it inside her right ear.

"Liz, Anne wants to know how you were able to mount your revolution inside the asylum that night." Clara's voice was a bit louder than her normally feminine and lilting softness.

Obviously deciding that this question was of major importance to the group, Elizabeth Packard stood up to address the assemblage, in the tradition of the elder generation, of whom she was such a noble exemplar. Clara's eyes filled with emotion as she listened to the woman's words. And, as she looked out at the members of her now close-knit group, she could see that their eyes, as well, were tearing up, and she could hear snuffles and sniffs coming from many of them.

"I know you might expect that I had some secret knowledge

of how to communicate with the insane mind. I did not. And, I do not have any such knowledge today. I simply spoke to my audience as one would address any fellow human on the planet. I used logic. Plain and simple logic. For, you see, what separates us humans from the animal kingdom is that we can communicate with everyone, despite our language differences, and even despite our mental differences. We do not seek to survive in some violent, tragic display of hatred and warfare, the way Mr. Galton describes his version of reality."

"His version was based on his egotistical outlook," Clara said.

Mrs. Packard nodded. "When I told those patients that the doctors were drugging them without their permission, they immediately knew they had to act. I have seen this response in many other asylums around the world. Humans want to be seen as thinking, moral beings, who can judge what is good for them, on their own, and not by being given chemicals to alter their thinking. I believe, you see, that the mind is one large chemical set, and we must be careful not to pollute it with outside ingredients, which can cause confusion and stress. Observe closely, a child concentrating in a meadow, who watches a butterfly winging its way around her. That child simply wants to behold the beauty of freedom in its natural environment. Mental patients want to also behold freedom, on their own, and they want to be able to work out their own problems, on their own. When I told Dr. Rooney that I work with each person's so-called insane world view, I meant it. Nothing is insane unless it becomes an obsession that keeps us from respecting one another. Most humans, even lunatics, understand that basic human fact. Those who would come between us, as thinking human beings, yearning for individual freedom, and respecting the rights of others, are forever seen as the true villains in our stories. My ladies acted because they wanted their freedom respected. And, if I have anything to say about it, they shall receive it!"

"Mrs. Foltz! There's a messenger here. It's an emergency telegram from Washington D. C." Joseph Hannigan, the butler, stood at the door to the library.

"Bring it forward, please," Clara said, wondering who would write to her from the nation's capitol.

The Western Union boy walked through the Library, glancing warily at the adults assembled therein. He received Clara's signature, and she took the telegram from him.

"Thank you," Clara said, and she read the message.

"I'm afraid it's bad news," she told the group. "It's from Miss Miriam Levine, the Attorney General's assistant. We met her during my first case, the Chinatown murders. She wants me to come to Washington immediately. The current appointee to the Supreme Court, Judge Marshal Owens, has been assassinated. She wants me to defend his assassin, who happens to be a woman."

Ah Toy, Laura, Trella, Bertha, Adeline and Samuel, all stood up in unison. "We will help you pack, mother," Trella told her.

From the back of the room, David Milton, age sixteen, spoke up. "Mother, I wish to help you as well this time."

Clara carefully folded the telegram and placed it inside her dress's top pocket. "Don't worry, we shall decide who assists in due time. Right now, I am going to wire Miss Levine to find out more information. As we know, without adequate information, the truth will never be discovered."

Next Mystery in the Portia of the Pacific Series

In San Francisco, attorney and detective Clara Foltz gets a telegram from the White House. Attorney General Augustus Hill Garland has appointed her to be the defense counsel for the accused murderess, Eloise Strong. Clara agrees to do it, and she is packing for Washington D. C. She is taking her partner, attorney Laura Gordon and her lover, Captain Isaiah Lees, and her next-to-youngest son, David Milton with her. Dr. Andrew McFarland, an alienist, is also going to be there to examine Miss Strong's mental capacity.

Here is the first chapter in the latest mystery in the Portia of the Pacific series, _The Angel's Trumpet_:

Chapter 1: Suffragette

Swampoodle Grounds, Washington, D. C., May 4, 1887.

Eloise Strong, at twenty-four, knew that her time was precious. She must obtain a recommendation from her lover, Marshal Owens, or she would never be admitted to law school. As she pushed and shoved her way through the crowds assembled at the ball park, her eyes focused on him, the tall red-haired gentleman standing near the Nationals' bench.

The Washington team was playing the Detroit Wolverines, who were in first place, so the stands were filled with a raucous assortment of cheering men. There was only one man Eloise wanted to see, and she was almost up to him when she felt a hand pulling on her left arm.

"Miss? Where do you think you're going?" A tall bearded man, in a maroon frock coat and striped britches, whose breath smelled of onion and garlic, was scowling down at her. He wore a black bowler with a scarlet cobra badge on the front. This meant he was one of the toughs who protected the illegal gambling going on amongst the mostly male spectators. Eloise assumed he was a gangster of some kind.

"I must talk to this gentleman," she said, pointing toward Marshal, who was now turning toward her, a confused look on his face under his brown gentleman's derby with the tiny pheasant feather in the band. Her lover was wearing brown corduroy trousers, and a matching topcoat, with a green velvet vest and a mink collar. He tugged at his reddish-brown, walrus mustache, which Eloise knew was a signal that he was quite irritated.

"What are you doing here?"

Marshal's fifty-five years showed in his wrinkled forehead and crow's feet, as he frowned at her. Eloise wondered why white men aged faster.

"May we talk?"

She took his arm. He had always been easy to persuade, from the first time she ushered him into the upper bedrooms of the Oyster Glen Restaurant on Massachusetts, where she worked.

They walked toward the Refreshment Tents, over by the first base side of the field.

Eloise knew Marshal was an Appellate Court Judge. He had never kept his professional life secret from her, and this was the main reason she was there. She had a unique chance to enroll in Harvard Law School, as its first Negro woman, but she needed his recommendation to allow her to bypass the usual scrutiny. Marshal had often remarked upon her astute legal mind, and he had encouraged her education, even if it had started late.

As they strolled into the shade of the tents, she could smell the odors of popped corn, oysters on the half shell, and grilled chicken and frankfurters.

"We had a guest speaker in Mrs. Terrell's class today. He plays in the International League for the Newark club. Moses Fleetwood Walker. Do you know him?"

She wanted to get Marshal in a good mood, and she knew he loved baseball.

"Yes. I do. There are still a few Negroes playing in that league. That will all be changing, however, at the end of this season."

He took out one of his Cuban cigars from the breast pocket of his top coat, bit off the end, and spat it onto the sawdust. The deep tone of Marshal's voice sounded negative as he lit his smoke and began to puff.

"The owners have informed us they will be preventing any race-mixing on teams beginning next season. Except for a few star players, who shall be grandfathered with old contracts, no new Negro will be allowed to play."

Eloise reached into her blue handbag and rummaged around for something. When she found it, she turned to face him. She watched, as his deep blue, privileged Welsh eyes roamed freely over her body.

She wore the new powder blue dress from Paris, with its tiny straw hat and blue satin band, and the matching handbag with silver clasps. He bought it for her on their anniversary. It had been a passionate relationship of fifteen months, filled with clandestine meetings in various hotels around Washington, but they had never, until that moment, been seen together in public.

"Mr. Walker will want to know that. He seemed to be optimistic about the future of our race in baseball. The sport, he said, was one of the few fields of endeavor where performance mattered more than birth privilege." She saw him smile, so she continued. "Except, he said, many of the white Southern boys seem to enjoy sliding into his catcher position at home plate with their metal cleats brandished like Confederate swords."

Marshal reached out to touch Eloise on her slender, alabaster nose, and moved down to caress his index finger on her equally thin pink lips. "Your genetics, thank goodness, allow you to mix rather well with the public." He reached around her head and grasped a lock of her tight black curls. "Except for your hair, which has also been grandfathered in, it seems."

"Has the Attorney General summoned you yet? The *Post* had an editorial by President Cleveland about why he chose you for the Supreme Court. Mrs. Terrell read it to our class. I was so proud of you!"

She brought her right hand out of the handbag and thrust it inside the crook of his left forearm, holding it there, her brown eyes gazing up at his face.

"What was it you wanted to ask?" Marshal gently took her arm away, and it fell limply to her side. "Honestly, my dear, it's rather reckless of us to be seen out here." He swiveled his head, from side-to-side, searching for anyone he recognized in the crowd.

"Why dangerous? You're known to be one of Washington's most available bachelors. You said I was equal to any woman you've ever met, in both intelligence and beauty."

Eloise recalled their long embraces and his frequent promises of adoration. Now, however, something had changed in his eyes. It was as if their long talks together had meant nothing.

Her lover bent forward, cupped his right hand up to his mouth, and whispered. She could feel the spray from his lips upon her cheeks. "I shall be on the highest court in the land. I cannot be seen with a bastard and former slave. Your outward appearance means nothing to those in my social circle. It is your breeding that matters. Just like your friend, Fleetwood Walker. There can be no more contracts with the major leagues, no matter how well you both play the game."

Her right hand, once more, reached down into her handbag. As her gaze riveted onto his, she could envision Moses Walker's face, as it superimposed over this stranger, this imposter lover.

Walker's lean, dark, and intelligent face, with flaring, wide nostrils, sensitive and bountiful lips, spoke the words she remembered. His father was a physician, a respected medical doctor. Eloise could hear his carefully enunciated speech coming from beneath that perfectly groomed mustache. What he had spoken in class now made this white man's swollen pink jowls and ugly scowl seem ludicrous in the bright sunshine.

Social inequality means that in all the relations that exist between man and man he is to be measured and taken not according to his natural fitness and qualification, but that blind and relentless rule, which accords certain pursuits and certain privileges to origin or birth.

169

When she finally spoke, her words sounded hollow and without passion.

"I can be accepted into Harvard Law School, where you graduated, Marshal. I simply need a single letter of recommendation. That's what Mr. Terrell told me. He, too, graduated from Harvard, and he believes I can be the first Negro woman to attend. Won't you allow me this chance? Doesn't our love, for all these months, mean anything to you?"

When Marshal began to lecture her, Eloise began to fantasize. She had done this many times before in her life. After the Civil War, in Virginia, she was eight years old, working in the plantation cotton fields as an emancipated slave and sharecropper. A white man came riding up on a black horse and addressed all of the workers, telling them they could live free and get free schooling in the nation's capital. She had dreamed then, along with the others, and so they made the journey across the Potomac and into the city. She had no other hope, as her mother had died during child birth, the year before, and her father, and former master, Patrick Sloan Wolsey, sold his property and moved to Texas, the last location of the Confederacy, before the war ended.

". . . and I can no longer see you. My responsibilities are to this great nation of ours, and my reputation is at stake . . ."

Marshal's voice continued to drone, on and on, just the way Mr. and Mrs. Terrell's voices had done, promising her that she could rise up, and become educated, in order to demonstrate to those powerful elite that freedom extended to those who advanced through hard work and study. Her sympathetic tears agreed with the fantasies of her elders, and they flooded her mind, blotting-out the reality of her daily life. She did work hard, she studied hard, and she improved her lot, even though she had to do it by selling her body to the prominent politicians who frequented the restaurant where she worked as a waitress.

". . . Attorney General Garland chose me because I was independent. I cannot become encumbered with the likes . . ."

Eloise tightened her grip on the object inside her handbag. The Preparatory High School for Negroes was also selling her a dream. She was the only one of those from the plantation who had tested high enough to gain entrance. Even so, she had to become a prostitute to earn sufficient money to stay in school. And now, the biggest fantasy of all had come into her life: the idea that she, a half-Negro and half-woman, could gain access to the most prestigious university in the world. All she needed was a single, signed letter from a white judge. The key to her future, the gentleman standing in front of her, lecturing her, telling her about the reality of this nation's collective dream, had become, for her, an existential nightmare.

He was now smiling, reaching out once more, to touch her lips with his white forefinger, and she fantasized about the painting on the wall of the Sistine Chapel she had seen in one of her textbooks. It was created by the Italian artist, Michelangelo, and the metaphor now seemed very prophetic to her. The naked white man, Adam, was reaching out to touch the white-bearded, white God's finger. And she, a woman who was also white, but in color only, was now being touched by a man who was her new master. But she had this master in her web.

Her eyes moved down to Marshal's chest. The dagger inside her handbag was released from its feminine lair, so she dropped the bag, and she thrust its silver blade, glinting wildly in the sunlight, into this Man-god's heart-of-no-heart. She kept her unwavering fist around the dagger's black handle, as he bled all over her forearm, and it was her turn to smile.

She could feel the last pulsations of his heart's dark chambers, vibrating on the dagger's handle, as the masculine crowd around her circled the falling man, who was now on his knees. She bent over with him, as he collapsed backward onto the sawdust, writhing in pain like a serpent, his derby rolling away. She kept her right hand glued upon the hilt of the dagger, until Marshal made his final, gasping argument on this Earth, to the gathered throng of sportsmen and gawkers encircling him.

"Why, Eloise? You are now doomed."

ABOUT THE AUTHOR

James Musgrave's work has been recently featured in *Best New Writing 2011*, Eric Hoffer Book Awards, Hopewell Press, Titusville, N.J. He was semi-finalist in the Black River Chapbook Competition, Fall, 2012. He was also in a Bram Stoker Award Finalist volume of horror fiction, *Beneath the Surface, 13 Shocking Tales of Terror*, Shroud Publishing, San Francisco, CA. His historical mystery series starring Detective Patrick James O'Malley was selected as "featured titles" by the American Library Association's Self-E Program for Independent Authors. The first mystery in that series, *Forevermore*, won the First-Place blue ribbon for Best Historical Mystery, in the Chanticleer International Clue Book Awards, 2013. James lives in San Diego, and is the publisher of EMRE Publishing, LLC.

Sign-up for the Author's Newsletter at emrepublishing.com